THE FAWN
AND
OTHER STORIES

I0606952

THE FAWN AND OTHER STORIES

THOMAS GRISSOM

SUNSTONE PRESS
SANTA FE

© 2020 by Thomas Grissom
All Rights Reserved
No part of this book may be reproduced in any form or by any electronic or mechanical means including information storage and retrieval systems without permission in writing from the publisher, except by a reviewer who may quote brief passages in a review.

Sunstone books may be purchased for educational, business, or sales promotional use.
For information please write: Special Markets Department, Sunstone Press,
P.O. Box 2321, Santa Fe, New Mexico 87504-2321.

Book and cover design › R. Ahl
Printed on acid-free paper
∞

Library of Congress Cataloging-in-Publication Data

Names: Grissom, Thomas, 1940- author.
Title: The fawn and other stories / by Thomas Grissom.
Description: Santa Fe : Sunstone Press, [2020] | Includes reader's guide. | Summary: "Stories of the human heart in conflict with itself as it struggles to resolve those human dilemmas that confront us in determining how we live our lives"-- Provided by publisher.
Identifiers: LCCN 2020026037 | ISBN 9781632933102 (paperback) | ISBN 9781611396041 (epub)
Subjects: LCGFT: Short stories.
Classification: LCC PS3607.R577 A6 2020b | DDC 813/.6--dc23

LC record available at https://lccn.loc.gov/2020026037

WWW.SUNSTONEPRESS.COM
SUNSTONE PRESS / POST OFFICE BOX 2321 / SANTA FE, NM 87504-2321 /USA
(505) 988-4418 / FAX (505) 988-1025

For Becky, yet again.

Contents

PREFACE

Some of the oldest examples of writing are stories told by early humans to explain the world, to try to make sense of it and understand their place in it. Storytelling leads ultimately to religion, history, philosophy, great literature, even science and speculations about the nature of the universe. As our understanding of the world has increased, the importance of stories has also grown. Stories allow us to freely examine those human experiences and dilemmas that confront, confound and confuse us in making the choices that determine how we understand and live our lives. Each story is a vignette of the human heart in conflict with itself as it struggles to resolve the choices we must make. Stories allow us to freely explore more than one level of meaning and more than one simple truth. They are created and live in the imagination and collective experiences of the writer. And they are all true, as true to our experiences as the writer knows how to make them. It is the task of the writer to get beyond facts. Facts are never the answer to any real question. Real questions don't have answers. That's what makes them questions. The simple facts of our existence are merely the stage on which the real truths are acted out and resolved, those truths depicted in the stories we tell, to explain the world to ourselves and make sense of it.

THE FAWN

The dog stopped at the far edge of the yard, just before entering the woods, and stood, motionless, looking back long at the house. For the second time that morning the man watched it out the window. All around the clearing grew a dense screen of red alder and blackberry vines, beyond which a stand of Douglas fir and hemlock rose high overhead. Earlier, the same dog had trotted out of the woods beside the house, and cautiously crossed the yard, before disappearing again into the underbrush at precisely the spot where it stood now, looking back over its shoulder.

He could see it was a hound of some sort, long-legged and thin, probably not very well cared for, and its dark, mottled coat blended into the perpetual half shadows that dotted the edge of the lawn. A silent tracker, the man thought to himself; one of those solitary hounds that hunt alone, never barking on a trail. No good for proper hunting, he remembered, unless perhaps you put them with a pack; but he's hunting nevertheless—that's the same track he was on earlier. If he's been around more than once, he thought, chances are he's on to something—or thinks he is.

"Here boy, here. Come 'ere, boy. Come on now—this way." A woman's voice pleaded from the narrow side yard beyond the corner of the house.

So she saw it too, he thought; he was afraid she might. He had not heard her stirring about the house once the rattling of the breakfast dishes ceased and he knew that on a morning like this one she would find some pretext for being outside. The woman was trying to coax the hound toward her and away from the woods. He knew that she was thinking of the fawn.

The man moved across the room to another window, from which he could see both the woman and the dog. In her outstretched hand the woman held some scraps of food. "Here boy, come on now," she pleaded.

The dog made no move to run away but the man knew that it wouldn't come to her either. The best she could hope for would be to keep it there awhile, and only then if she didn't try to approach too close. Such dogs are naturally aloof when they are hunting, he thought, and distance themselves from everything. They get so accustomed to being alone they don't like having anyone come near. Perhaps there is some premonition of the kill—something about the anticipation of catching another animal and tearing it to pieces—that makes them more wary than at other times. Strike dogs didn't seem so, he recalled; they're so hell-bent on chasing something and bellowing out their excitement that they are oblivious to everything. He knew that truly good trackers behaved the same. They simply put their noses to the ground and followed a scent, and on a hot trail one of them could pass literally within reach and seem unaware you were even there. He recalled an incident one night long ago at the pond in his father's pasture. He had been hunting bullfrogs, and he had just fired his .22 rifle at a pair of eyes shining on the far bank when he heard a rustling and caught sight in his light of a gray fox running along the fence beside the pond and out across the mown field beyond. The fox couldn't have been more than ten yards away when he first spotted it, and he watched it for as long as he could still see it in the flashlight beam. Then he switched off the light to wait and listen for the hounds. Fully five minutes later two of them came down the same path the fox had taken. Neither uttered a sound nor deviated in the least when he flicked on the light, oblivious to everything but the invisible chemical trail left by the fox in the wet grass. In his mind he watched them again, disappearing in the dim light, swallowed up by the darkness and the decades in between. But there were other dogs—neither such good trackers nor strike dogs—that trailed silently, largely by sight he guessed, and which would go out of their way to avoid any contact on the chase. Maybe they are the killers, he thought, and not without shame for what they do. He knew that they could be relentless on a trail and indefatigable in the pursuit of their quarry.

He had a dog like that himself once, when he was growing up. It simply wandered up one day from who knows where. His father told him it wouldn't stay, to head off the boy's disappointment, but he fed it, and after leaving once or twice it finally took up around the place. The boy took it hunting with him whenever he went out after rabbits or squirrels, but the old dog never showed much interest in anything but running foxes at night in the bottomland and wooded hollows along the river, and of course deer, and even then you didn't know when he was on a trail because he didn't have a trail voice. When he tracked, he was completely silent.

"They's jest some dogs like that," old man Trundle told him. "Mostly solitary dogs, they is; they prefers their own comp'ny, and they's got their own ways 'bout 'em." "Humpy" Trundle was generally acknowledged to have the best fox hounds in those parts, and to a young boy growing up he knew more about the ways of dogs than anyone would ever likely know again. Years later, long after he had grown up and become sophisticated, he would still marvel at what the old man understood of dogs and hunting. "You don't wanna try to git too close to 'em," he had cautioned the boy; "they's too independent for that. If you try to make a pet out of 'em, they'll only leave and move on to take up some'eres else, where they can own more freedom. And don't never think you can train one of 'em to be no different somehow. By the time you recognizes what you're dealin' with, it's too late for that; 'bout the most you can hope for is some sorta understandin'."

And that's what he and the old dog had. He took him along whenever he went hunting but once in the field the old hound would go his own way and kept his distance. The only time he showed any real excitement was when he would jump a deer out of one of the thickets along the creek and go tearing after it, bounding over the open fields toward the sanctuary of the big woods. It was the only chance the boy ever got to see the dog at work, because he would invariably follow the deer on out of sight, or off into the woods, and be gone for days. Occasionally in the evenings he would notice the dog quivering with excitement as he tested the air with his nose, and he knew that he smelled a fox or a deer moving about at dusk, and afterwards the dog would trot off through the pasture not to come back before morning, sometimes not for days. His father's neighbors reported seeing the dog chasing deer in their fields or pastures and often when he was gone for a long time they would get reports from all over, once from as far away as Mutton Hollow over in Sevier County. The local fox hunters claimed that he sometimes ran with their dogs too.

The foxhounds ran mostly at night, although sometimes they would stay out for days at a time as one trail grew cold or crossed another, and one race died out and another one resumed. These hollows were full of foxes, both the hardier gray foxes and the more cunning red ones, many of which had been imported by the local hunters from breeders in other states and turned loose here to provide sport for the hounds. Every Friday evening about dusk, year round during good weather, the hunters would meet at one of several designated points along the roads that crisscrossed the hills and farmlands, bringing their hounds with them in kennels mounted on the backs of pickup trucks, or on trailers pulled behind, to form up a pack, usually more than one, and release the dogs at just about the time it was getting too dark to see clearly. The hounds, at least those that survived this business, enjoyed it even more than their handlers and would come boiling out of the wire mesh cages to quickly disappear into the surrounding brush. Within a few hundred yards or so, one of the strike dogs, aptly designated, would cross a scent stronger and more distinct than the profusion of other musky odors hanging on the evening air and erupt in an excited, throaty bawl that brought the other dogs squalling and signaled the start of a race.

"That's Bell," Humpy Trundle would holler, and the hunt was on, in a chorus of such urgent and feverish bellowing and barking that it always made the hair on the back of the boy's neck stand on end. Someone would make a fire, and the men sat around in folding chairs or on stools or milk crates or whatever else they had brought to sit on and listened to the hounds run the fox. It wasn't always a fox they were chasing, but generally it was, and the hunters could quickly tell the difference anyway between a race involving a fox and one in which the dogs were only chasing a deer or a coon. A deer would rapidly outdistance its pursuers and lead them well out of hearing, whereas a coon would soon "tree" and the sound of the dogs barking would become stationary and take on a desultory tone of indifference. A fox on the other hand would keep just in front of the hounds, running a route that by now the hunters recognized and could use to identify specific individuals who always ran the same pattern time after time. Gray foxes were able to climb and would sometimes escape by scrambling up the slanting trunk of a partially downed or misshapen tree, or else would elude the hounds by "going to ground" in a rocky outcropping or in a den in the ground or hollow log, or beneath the roots of an old tree somewhere. For that reason red foxes were the desired quarry, preferring instead to keep moving ahead of the hounds and leading races that often went on for hours and would surge in and out of hearing several times in the course of a single evening. The wiliest individuals of the red species appeared to enjoy the challenge as much as the hounds, following a circuit clearly of the fox's choosing and seeming to toy with the pursuers along the way. These races would end abruptly at some point when the fox, usually by doubling back on its own trail for a ways, would give the dogs the slip and escape, sometimes to be encountered again somewhere else in the same night, which the hunters could tell by the particular way each fox ran in front of the pack. One red fox is worth a whole den of grays, one of the men would grumble; but the red fox was a particular and discriminating resident and over the years had not fared as well in competition with people as the more resilient gray species. In the last analysis any fox would do, so long as there were good hounds to chase it and open spaces available for the race.

During the evening someone would pass a bottle around, and there would be time to catch up on all the local news and gossip. For most of these men it was the primary social event of their lives, this sitting around in the evening, visiting, reminiscing and listening to the hounds run. It was fox hunting, Tennessee style, and it bore no resemblance to the way it was done in the hunt country of Virginia or Maryland where the hunters dressed up in livery and rode to the hounds along a trail established by a rider on horseback pulling a scented drag, in a ritual that these hunters would have disdained to the same degree that they would not have understood it. To them, theirs was the gentlemanly form of fox hunting, where the hounds were the center of attention, and where the reward was the relaxed companionship of other hunters basking in the light of a pleasant fire, with a pipeful of homegrown tobacco and a nip or two from a bottle to accompany the music of the hounds. It was how the man, as a boy, had learned about hunting and it was still for him the standard by which he continued to measure all hunting.

Even before he had a dog, the boy joined the circle around the fire. The first few times his father had accompanied him, to break the ice, but Humpy Trundle had taken a liking to the boy right off and from the beginning everyone was given to understand that he was welcome. Still, the boy realized his place and was content to sit quietly and listen to the hounds and to the men. At first, the men could hear the dogs, or said they did, where the boy heard only silence or the normal sounds of the night. "Which one is that now, Mr. Trundle?" one of the younger men would ask and the old man would offer an opinion as to whether the faint sound which the boy could only try to imagine was Bell or Susy or Blue or one of the other dogs released earlier that evening, or whether in fact he claimed he could hear all of them. To make matters worse, on any given evening there were usually several packs of hounds released, each at a different place about the surrounding countryside, and the hunters at each of the release sites could listen to all the other races too, so that there might be as many as fifty dogs running at the same time.

In the beginning the boy doubted the men could always hear the hounds, or even if they could that they could distinguish one from the other by the faint sounds. Then, gradually, the boy too could pick the sounds of the barking dogs out of the background noise of wind and tree frogs and the faint hum of traffic on a distant highway. It was, he found, a matter of expecting to hear it, and once he expected to then he began to hear them where before he had not heard anything. Little by little, by listening to the hounds and to the men talk about them, he learned to identify specific individuals and to recognize them not just by their voices but by their behavior on the trail as well. How Bell could always be counted on to strike a trail first, or to find it again when it grew cold, but how after that Blue would quickly outdistance the other members of the pack and seemed to have a special sense about which direction the fox would go, and how Susy always ran well back in the pack, and how Whitey, one of her pups, stayed right beside her, and so on, how each of the foxhounds performed as the race unfolded.

The boy never felt as confident or as sure of himself as the men seemed to, but he no longer doubted much of what they said though he was not always convinced. There were occasional disagreements among them too, for which Humpy Trundle served as the final arbiter. The old man mostly remained silent, just listening, and stayed above the dispute, as the acknowledged patriarch of the group. He had good hounds, and he understood dogs and foxes and hunting, and men too, and he used his position wisely, with the calm good judgment the others had come to recognize and respect. Most of them had at one time or another relied on his judgment in the matter of foxhounds, and in other matters as well, and he had helped many of them get their start. Whenever they turned to him for his opinion he offered it freely, and they in turn accepted it without question. Even if they might have disagreed it was more important to preserve the harmony of the group and to uphold the old man's authority for the next time, when he would perhaps agree with them. Someone would simply change the subject and the discussion would move on to something else.

The boy came home promptly every Friday after school—declining the inevitable invitations and the many distractions that accompanied the end of another school week and the anticipation of the weekend with two whole days of no classes—and went straight to his chores, to honor the unspoken but mutually understood agreement he had with his father about being allowed to join the hunters. Afterwards, whatever time remained before supper, he spent in his room doing homework. He made certain he was there when his mother came to call him to the table, his head buried in a book. He let himself be called more than once before finally slamming his book shut, loud enough to be heard, and taking his place at the table.

His mother was a woman who regarded any excess with a wary suspicion. It was alright to like a thing, but whenever it became a passion she viewed it as potentially corrupting and a dangerous contradiction to the concept that life was not frivolous. To her the worthwhile endeavors were those requiring a certain amount of discipline, which one did primarily for the good of one's soul and not out of desire. The boy realized that it would not do to appear too eager to go fox hunting. Whenever any activity became a regular occurrence his mother's instinctive suspicions were aroused and she automatically policed it.

Fortunately for the boy the men did not hunt every week, not during fall and winter when school was going on and it was often raining, or the weather turned off freezing and bitter cold or the wind blew too hard and the hounds couldn't hold the scent, and even if they did the men couldn't hear them anyway. During long spells of bad weather the hunters had been known to erect a tin-roofed lean-to for shelter against the rain, and to build a roaring fire to combat the cold, in order to find at least one night's relief a week from the boredom of no hunting and give the dogs a chance to work off the excess energy that otherwise they expended in fighting and injuring each other, which occasionally even resulted in money having to be spent on a veterinarian. But you couldn't hear the hounds above the crackle of a roaring fire or even a light drizzle on a tin roof, or the boy couldn't; even after he learned to hear the dogs well he still couldn't fool himself into believing that he could hear them above the fire and the steady drum of rain on a sheet of tin, so this was hunting merely to be going through the motions and the boy skipped those sessions without regret. Besides, it was good politics and helped ensure harmony with his mother, who knew the hunters were sitting alongside the road in the rain and considered them certainly foolish if not completely daft because of it. But it seldom rained in the summer and the hunters could be counted on to be there every Friday evening. By then school was out for summer vacation and his mother did not consider it inappropriate that the boy should, for that brief period of time, want to indulge in what, during the more serious portion of the year, she would have considered excessive. Still, the boy did not want to arouse her suspicions by appearing too eager. He knew that if he did, not even his father would be able to help him.

Although she never said so, the boy knew his mother considered fox hunting something that men did only after they were too old to be really productive anymore; or after they had gotten too set in their ways to talk sense to and it was simply better to tolerate a foolish but relatively harmless indulgence like fox hunting than contend with trying to change behavior that if opposed might show up in some even more foolish and potentially harmful activity. Not everyone liked being kept awake by the barking of hounds until the slack hours of the morning and his mother was one of those. There was enough open countryside and too few hounds for the barking dogs to remain long within hearing, unless of course the fox treed or went to ground, or the dogs got off on a coon trail and it happened to tree near a farmhouse. Then those hounds in the pack whose nature it was to bark "treed" would take over and the barking would assume the incessant and repetitious tone of an audible beacon, directed to those hunters who even if within hearing were firmly rooted to their chairs or camp stools or logs around the fire and had no interest in any fox holed-up and not still running free, and no interest whatsoever in any coon or anything else that climbs trees, and who at any rate were never summoned by the long and sonorous and eventually doleful "treed" barking of the dogs. Relief came only when the hounds finally lost interest or one of the strike dogs in the pack struck a new trail, or the same trail going back in the other direction, and by its short, choppy, insistent bawls convinced the other hounds that the prospect of this new chase held greater urgency than sitting around in the dwindling hopes that whatever was holed-up might suddenly reappear.

On occasion some dog would refuse to give up and would continue to bark treed for hours. That happened one night down by the tulip poplar that grew in his father's front pasture along the riverbank, and his mother had complained. That time, his father took the 12-gauge out to the patio and sprayed shot through the leafy upper branches of the tree. The booming eruption of sound, directed toward the dogs and shattering the stillness of the night, startled them and scared them off. The next day his father made certain to assure Humpy Trundle that he had not been shooting at the hounds but at a skunk which had been making a nuisance of itself by eating the leftover food scraps they put out each day for the cat. The boy knew his father would not shoot the dogs, and the fox hunters knew it too, but it was nice to be reassured because they also knew that some others did. Whenever one of the dogs failed to return there was always the suspicion that someone whose land they crossed on their inevitable wanderings after the fox had killed it. Sometimes one of the dogs would come back with lead shot embedded under its skin.

The night the boy had stood in the pasture at the edge of the stock pond and seen first the fox and then the two dogs go by, he realized afterwards that the fox hunters might suspect the shots were directed toward the hounds and not just at bullfrogs. So when a few minutes later he noticed a flashlight in the front pasture, he reasoned that this time the sound of rifle fire had brought them out looking for their dogs or for whoever was doing the shooting. Concerned, yet cautious about what he might be walking into, the boy screwed up his courage and made his way in the dark down the hill toward where he could see the dim light swinging about in the tall grass.

When he reached the fence at the edge of the field he discovered there two men. The one nearest him with the light was wading through the thick grass toward the woods that stretched along the riverbank on the other side of the pasture, where earlier that evening the boy had heard dogs barking. The second man, about two hundred yards behind the first, appeared to be caught in the barbed wire that separated the pasture from the woods beyond, and was cursing to himself in the dark. The man with the light yelled for the other man to hurry.

The boy slipped through the fence and plunged into the tangled fescue that had grown up higher than his waist. The man with the light heard him and turned in the boy's direction. "Who's there?" he called. "Wait up," the boy said. When he reached the man, the boy recognized him as Luke Latham's nephew who lived in the Seven Islands Community a few miles up the river. Luke was one of the fox hunting regulars and his nephew had a reputation as something of a wheeler-dealer when it came to buying and selling hunting dogs. The boy hadn't seen him in the select circle of hunters before. But the other men often mentioned him, some with a sort of grudging admiration for this dog or that one with which he had been involved at one time or another, some with an uneasy but polite suspicion, but virtually all with a skeptical note of familiarity that kept the boy from deciding exactly what was being implied.

Quickly he explained that the shooting the man had heard was only the boy hunting bullfrogs. The man appeared to take no interest in what the boy was saying. "Where are we anyway?" he asked, then said, "I wish to hell he'd keep up." The boy told him he was on the Johnston place and that this was his father's field. "Damn. I knew it," the man swore. "I been lost for the last hour. What with tryin' to keep track of him and those dogs too," he said, "it's a wonder I ain't broke my leg stumblin' around out here in the dark. I'm gittin too old for this."

The boy saw that the man's arms were scratched and bleeding. His shirt was torn, and he was sweating from the exertion of walking through the thickly clumped grass. "Hurry up," the man called again to his companion. By now the other man had freed himself from the fence and was moving slowly toward them. "Have you seen any dogs?" the first man asked, as if nothing the boy said had registered.

"Oh, yes," the boy answered, "and it was just the prettiest sight you ever saw." Thinking to reassure the man and bolster his spirits, he described the scene with the fox and the dogs at the pond, how the fox had come out of the woods from the same direction as the men but had run up the hill along the fence, and how the two hounds had followed the same track, noses to the ground, making every single turn the fox had taken, in what the boy was sure proved their prowess as foxhounds.

"Shhh, quiet!" the man suddenly hissed, looking back to where his companion was struggling through the hip-high grass. "I'm tryin' to sell him one of those dogs as a coonhound," he whispered, lowering his voice and taking the boy into his confidence. "They ain't supposed to be runnin' no fox. Don't say nothin' 'bout that," he pleaded, treating the boy now with the respect due an equal. "They's considerable money ridin' on it. I'll do one for you sometime," the man promised, then muttered half under his breath, "Damn. Maybe I'm makin' a mistake sellin' that dog. You say he was right behind that fox, huh? Dog like that might oughta bring more." The boy promised to say nothing, and retreated.

He never betrayed the confidence, though he never profited from it either, but afterwards he wondered just how much the fox hunters knew about what the dogs were trailing when they sat around listening and discussing among themselves how this dog or that one was doing on the chase. To the boy it wasn't important. He loved to listen to the hounds, and for that matter to the men too. It was enough to know that they were indeed chasing something, which could have been a fox or coon or deer or bobcat, or even a rabbit for all he cared, and to hear the urgency in their voices and the swift progress of the race through the quiet countryside at night. To know that wild things were still running free and leading other wild things, domesticated by man but wild nevertheless, and never completely rid of that instinct to hunt and to pursue their quarry and eventually to kill if they could, the way wild dogs had always done and the way he hoped that wolves still did if there were any wolves left anywhere, on the kind of pursuit that for the boy then—and for the man still—signified the ineluctable, undeniable mystery of the world. It stirred something deep inside him which he had never been able to adequately express or completely comprehend; but which he refused to deny because it affirmed the struggle he observed everywhere around him, and which he recognized instinctively as the one fundamental truth.

"It has become a struggle out of control, and out of context," the boy's father once told him. But any struggle was at some point one-sided, he knew. Until something takes over, some advantage is gained, and brings it back into balance. He only knew that it spoke to him in a way nothing else did. He hoped he would never have to face a world without wildness, domesticated to the point where it was no longer possible to sit and listen to hounds barking in pursuit of some wild thing fleeing in the night. Sure the dogs were capable of killing, and would too, if given the chance. The dog which a few hours before he had petted and scratched behind the ears and which had nuzzled and sniffed his hand in fond recognition might become a snarling, tearing beast obeying an instinct far more remote than the one which allied it to man. And the fox had to deal with that, in the best way it could. That was part of what it meant to be a fox, in a world in which there were also men and foxhounds. Before that, there had been other predators, other risks. The dogs also took their chances; in the dark, against the roads with speeding cars, and the barbed wire fences and uncovered cisterns, the abandoned mine shafts and natural crevices in the limestone hills, and the occasional disgruntled person who shot at them. The boy saw no fear in their eyes, only a sort of calm indifference, the same look he imagined he would find in the eyes of the fox. The men took their chances too, against the rules and regulations and contrivances of society; and against the very progress and success and obstinacy of man himself which each year made it seem less and less likely that there would always be fox hunting in these hills.

The boy recalled how the men had told him one evening of the caretaker at Huffaker's Ferry on the French Broad river, who years before had borne a grudge about something that no one even remembered anymore, and who as a result began shooting their dogs whenever he got a chance. The ferry was situated near a broad stretch of bottomland at the mouth of Gap Creek. The hunting there was good and the dogs ran there often. Over a period of many months the men lost one dog after another. Each one he killed the caretaker bound with baling wire, to which he fastened a heavy stone, then dumped the carcass from the ferry in the middle of the river. It took almost a year for the hunters to confirm what they already suspected and to pull up several of the carcasses from the river bottom with grappling hooks, but before they could take any action the caretaker disappeared. When the new bridge was completed shortly afterwards the old ferry was abandoned. About the same time a movie company bought it to use in a major film production. In one scene the ferry was set on fire and put adrift in the river to capsize on the rocks. When the burned-out hulk was retrieved the decomposed body of the caretaker was found carefully wired to the bottom of the hull.

Perhaps someday there will be no more foxes, he thought. And no more dogs or people either. But he couldn't accept that, and he certainly wouldn't behave in any way that made it seem more likely that he did. He found it difficult to think about such things. He only knew that for now he wanted to hunt while he still could, before the struggle became too unbalanced one way or the other, too far out of context, and some new unforeseen advantage surfaced to take control, something ominous which at times he could almost sense but which he couldn't—wouldn't—accept.

After supper, without waiting to be asked, the boy helped his mother clear the dishes from the table and began washing them while she put away the leftovers. Then he wiped the table and the counter tops clean. Through the open window he heard the first sound of barking that told him the men had released the hounds. Good, the hunters are just at the top of the hill, he thought. After the dishes were dried he stood outside listening. He could barely hear the dogs at all, and he knew they had gone in the direction of the rich bottomland that lay on the other side of the ridge running between his father's place and the old Huffaker Ferry. There was lots of room over there, and on those nights when the dogs went that direction they would often stay out of hearing for long periods. But foxes were plentiful there and the boy knew he would hear several good races before the evening was over.

He stepped into the living room and announced that he was going to walk up the lane to the road and on up the hill to see how the hunt was progressing. Before his mother could speak, his father looked up and grunted his approval. "I'm almost through with my homework for Monday," the boy told his mother. "I can finish it easy tomorrow, so I won't have to do it on Sunday." She made no comment, which for her was tantamount to approval, and the boy left.

On the way out he slipped one of his father's pipes from the cluttered pipe rack on the pantry shelf. His father never used them anymore. He felt perfectly safe taking one since he knew he was not likely to be discovered. The boy didn't have enough courage yet to drink their whiskey, but one of the hunters would always offer him a pipeful of tobacco. The boy would light up the pipe, and in the clouds of smoke which resulted from trying to keep it lit he hoped to obscure the differences that so obviously separated him from the older, more experienced men. The men would not tell on him, no more than his father might already have suspected, and the boy was careful not to abuse his privilege.

He could see the glow of the fire long before he reached the top of the hill. A row of empty dog pens lined the ditch bank alongside the road. The men were gathered at their usual station around a small fire in a hickory grove. When the boy reached them he unfolded the lawn chair he was carrying under one arm and silently took his place in the shadows, where he would not have to be too visible. By listening to the conversation he learned that a total of thirty-five or forty hounds in three different groups had been released that evening. But at the moment he could hear not a single one. He couldn't say whether the men heard anything or not because they were discussing something else and only mentioned the dogs occasionally, and then only in the abstract. The other two packs had been released in the adjoining hollow, separated from his father's farm by the sharp hogback ridge on which they sat and which the road crossed at this point. At each of the other release sites another group of hunters, the owners of the dogs turned loose there, had taken up their stations.

An hour passed, by which time the boy had lit his pipe, and trying not to be too obvious about it, was attempting to keep it going but in doing so was puffing great clouds of smoke that made him uncomfortably conspicuous, and during all that time he still had not heard the hounds. The men were discussing Luke Latham's nephew, who it seems had sold a young inexperienced coonhound for two hundred dollars one week only to buy it back the next for a hundred dollars more and sell it again a week later as a foxhound for even more money.

"Did he paint him first?" one of the men asked.

"Maybe that's why that new dog of yours barks 'treed' all the time, Luke," another one suggested.

"Them's utility dogs, sure enough" one of the men said. "Prob'ly got a knob hidden there somewhere on the nose, where you just dial up fox or coon or whatever you want. Wouldn't mind havin' me one of them dogs," he said, "if'n I could get it a right smart cheaper'n that."

The boy wanted to tell what he knew, and someday, he thought, perhaps he would. But for now he was content to remain silent and to feel a certain satisfaction at the secret knowledge that only he possessed. If he told them how it had happened he would only lose whatever advantage he held, and the boy had too few chits at this point to play them out casually. While he was still thinking about it, he suddenly became aware that he could hear the hounds. Their barking was like little faint explosions in the night air, tiny pinpricks of sound in his ears; heard from this distance there was a musical quality about it that reminded him of hearing a deep brass bell from far away.

"There they are," he announced, and cupped both hands behind his ears. That way he had discovered he could hear them as far as anyone, and now with cupped hands he was barely able to pick out of the mixed chorus the sound of several dogs whose voices he recognized. Bell was unmistakable. Her deep-throated bawl was the loudest and most insistent in the pack. Once or twice he imagined he could hear the short, choppy bark of Susy, who beat out a constant cadence until the race heated up and she became excited, after which she would start missing every third beat. Among the other sounds and obscuring much of them he could discern the feverish voice of Dan, one of the young dogs who didn't bark so much as he emitted a continuous, high-pitched squall, interrupting it only as necessary to catch his breath. The others, and these too most of the time, were merely a jumble of faint noises which he couldn't quite sort out or hear for long enough to make any judgment about what he was hearing, beyond thinking that occasionally he could identify these three.

The men sat quietly, straining to hear the chase. Now and then could be heard the slow sizzle of spittle, accompanied by the cherry red glow of a pipe in the dark. At regular intervals someone would break the quiet with a comment uttered almost unconsciously, and to no one in particular, before lapsing back into silence. The barking of the dogs was still too faint to hear above sustained conversation. They sat listening for what seemed a long time. After it became apparent that the dogs were not getting any closer the conservation turned to the question of where they were running and of what was happening at the other end of the barely audible sounds far off in the distance.

In his mind the boy had a picture of the pack strung out behind the leader, which he knew by this time would be Bubba or Blue or one of the other males that combined the speed and stamina with the nose and the experience to move fast while staying on the scent—Bell would not be far behind, and with her better nose could be counted on to strike the trail anew whenever the faster dogs in their headlong rush overran it—followed closely by the dozen or so others, at the rear of which ran the young hounds that were not so much chasing the fox but the rest of the pack as they mimicked the more experienced dogs in the process of learning how to hunt; of which some would never be anything more than followers since in any pack there were seldom more than three or four good hunting dogs that could be counted on to strike the trail and follow it until they lost it then strike it again, leading the rest of the pack along with them in a frenzied chorus of excited barking; and the boy could picture them plunging through the tall Johnson grass lining the edges of the cultivated fields and the ditch banks, hurtling through barbed wire fences down a creek bank and up the other side and finally out of sight in a thicket of willows and sycamores as the chase reached the edge of the woods along the river or swept up the hills overlooking the fertile farmland. He imagined it like a camera, focused on and panning with the dogs—Bell was the one that usually came to mind—the background flashing by in a confused blur as the hounds plunged through the brush or swept across the open spaces. Sometimes he imagined the old solitary dog instead, running silently in long smooth strides the way the boy had seen him chasing deer across the open fields, trailing by sight when he could and relying on his nose when forced to.

"Them dogs must've treed by now, way they's holdin' to one place," one of the men broke in.

"Not exceptin' Bell barks treed," objected another.

"Could be that's Russell Newman's bitch Ruby, instead of Bell," said the first. "She was in that bunch turned loose over at the school section.

"Naw, they's still on a trail, just ain't goin' nowhere," someone else added. "I figger in that wooded bottom beyond the ridge—over to the Kyker place, judgin' from the sound of it. Be mighty hard to hear 'em in there."

"Could be they's runnin' along the next ridge, keepin' the same distance from us all the time," the first man said.

The speculation continued. Finally no one else spoke, except one of the younger men who only had one dog in the pack and that a young, inexperienced bitch and who thought he could hear her occasionally and was looking for some confirmation from the others but didn't get it. The men settled back into silence to listen some more. The boy too sat listening, concentrating on the faint sounds and thinking about all the men had said, until, without thinking, he blurted out, "Where are they, Mr. Trundle?"

Until now the old man had kept silent. He took from his pocket a battered briar pipe with a well-chewed plastic stem chipped on the end where he held it in his teeth, filled it from a worn leather pouch, tamped it carefully, then lit it and puffed copious clouds of dense white smoke before answering.

"Them's our dogs, all right," he began. "I can hear Susy stutterin' ever time that fox let's 'em get close, and then there's Dan and Mike and Lucy. Russell's young bitch just ain't got the voice Bell does, and she could never keep up with Bell; not that she ain't a good'un—I ain't sayin' that—but there's only one Bell. She's been right up at the front of that race the whole time, which means that fox is runnin' round on 'em. I know that'un. Hit's that big gray we've chased before." He puffed on the pipe to keep it from going out, then continued. "Right now they're down in that cornfield in Summers Kelly's bottom, the one that lays just in below the ridge where the road crosses it again. There's fifty, sixty acres in that piece o'ground. That fox'll run 'round down in there fer quite a spell, cuttin' back and forth 'cross its trail to throw the hounds off the scent. Bell'll puzzle it out though, and when she does that fox'll come up out of there, go 'cross the road and over the ridge to the other side, where the dogs'll lose it in those woods out behind the church cemetery." He paused to suck on his pipe, before adding, "They's a den in one of them outcroppin's somewhere in there, but I ain't never been able to find it."

When the old man finished speaking the other men and the boy listened again for the hounds, this time with new interest, each one turning over in his thoughts what had been said. The boy was always surprised by the precision and the sense of certainty with which the old man purported to know what the hounds, which were so far away the boy could barely hear them, were doing. He no longer doubted that the old man could distinguish the sound of each dog since the boy himself was beginning to be able to identify some of them. But this was a countryside laid out in a patchwork of fields and woods, bottomland and numerous small hollows separated by low wooded ridges, with nooks and crannies extending in every direction. The number of possibilities for where the dogs could be was too great for the boy to understand how the old man could possibly know, by sitting here, where they were. "Because he has chased every fox in these hills at least a dozen times," his father had told him. "He knows each one by name, and what they will do, the same way he knows each dog and how it will behave, the same way you understand your mother and how she will react if you don't bring home a decent report card or go to Sunday School."

The boy had long since learned that his father possessed the same kind of wisdom which he had come to recognize in the old man; which he saw in the circumspect manner of his father toward his mother, managing to achieve his own modest ends and promoting those of the boy himself to participate in the normal activities of growing up while staying carefully within the limits prescribed by her, to the mutual satisfaction and benefit of all; which the boy believed he too possessed in some small measure and wanted to believe he would someday acquire in even greater store, as part of the legacy bequeathed him by his growing up in this place and time, in this land, among these people. The boy wanted to believe the old man was right, that he could be right. But he realized there were also limits—there were always limits—to what even the old man could know when he heard him describing the scene depicted by the faint sounds in the night air.

At length the younger man with the inexperienced dog spoke up. "Luke, I need to stretch a bit. Since that race is 'long side the road, what say we hop in my truck and drive up there—see how that pup of mine is doin'. Anyone care to go?" Luke and two others got up to go with him. The boy asked permission to ride in the back and climbed in. Then two more of the men climbed in with him.

It was three miles by the road before they reached the place where the road climbed out of the river valley up the ridge overlooking Summers Kelly's farm. As they neared it the boy could see another group of men standing around a pickup parked on the graveled shoulder near the top of the ridge. They pulled to a stop behind it and one of the men came walking back to where they were.

"You fellers should'a been here a few minutes ago," he said. "There was the damnedest race goin' on down there in that cornfield. That fox led them dogs back and forth 'tween here and the river I don't know how many times 'fore comin' up the hill and 'cross the road—and us standing right there watchin' the whole time."

"Where'd they go?" Luke asked.

"The dogs took across the ridge and out of hearin'," the other man responded. "You should'a seen it. When that fox came up out of there Bell and Bubba warn't fifty yards behind and closin' fast. Big gray one. Saw it clear in the headlights. Helluva good race."

The men sat listening to see if they could pick up any sound of where the dogs had gone. Then starting the truck they followed the road to the top of the ridge where it forked and went both ways, and took the direction that headed toward the Primitive Baptist Church. When they reached it they found several dogs milling about inside the low-walled church yard. In one corner stood an old cemetery with names that signified the Scottish and English ancestry of those who had settled here, on the weathered headstones dates going back almost two hundred years to when this had been the site of an earlier church with no name except that of "the church." When they turned off the engine the sound of a single hound barking treed could be heard coming from the woods beyond the cemetery. The rest of the dogs sniffed about aimlessly which signified that the fox had won this round. While they sat and listened Bell struck another scent. Immediately Dan, then, one by one, all the other hounds erupted in a continuing explosion of sound, and within a couple of hundred yards another chase was underway.

On the ride back the boy sat in the open bed of the truck with the cold night air blowing through his hair and against his face, causing little streams of tears to run from the corners of his eyes across his cheeks and into his ears, and thought: perhaps the old man isn't always right, but sometimes he is, and for the boy that was good enough. To the boy there was a truth to what the fox and the dogs were doing; and for the men just sitting there and listening there could also be a truth, and it resided in what the old man knew about such things, about the ways of hounds and foxes and in being able to understand that, also about the ways of men and the world and life in general; and although he did not yet understand all he felt about it the boy knew that this was a truth to cling to as certain as any and better than most they had tried to teach him. Perhaps it was not something you could ever hope to understand or try to explain to someone else, but that didn't keep it from being true, or keep him from knowing it. He would continue to have doubts when the men talked about the dogs and the chase, but they would be doubts based on a respect for what the old man knew about such matters, and for what the boy hoped to know too someday.

All hunters are liars about some things, at one time or another, the man knew; and he had known it back then too, but again it didn't matter, because as he got older he came to realize the elusive nature of any truth and the difficulty of separating out the truth from the larger store of traditional wisdom and assorted beliefs by which men conduct themselves and order their affairs; until eventually the only truth left is the emasculated, ephemeral truth of the philosophers which he thought had never been of any use to anyone; or the simple, uncomplicated truths like running foxes with hounds at night while sitting around a fire sipping whiskey and swapping tales in the company of others who understood without having to ask, or even think about it, what compelled you to want to do so; and he had already begun to realize it as soon as he took his place in that little circle of men gathered around the fire.

When they returned, Luke reported to the others what they had found. While they listened, the boy watched the old man puffing contentedly on his pipe. Only one question was raised, and that had to do with whether the trail Bell struck at the churchyard was made by another fox or merely the same one sneaking out of where it had treed earlier. There were several foxes that denned in that area, Humpy Trundle told them; most likely it was a new scent, laid down earlier, and that seemed to settle it. By then the men were engrossed in another race which had swung closer until now it too could be plainly heard.

And so the evenings passed, in quiet conversation, the dogs at times out of hearing for long periods during which the fire would be tended and the bottle passed around to rekindle spirits and relieve the boredom, until finally someone would pick up the distant bell-like sounds of hounds on the trail and attention would swing back to the chase. Some of these hunts lasted all night with the last survivors sticking around until dawn to pick up whatever hounds happened to come straggling in, expecting to be fed. The hunters left the portable kennels at the release site with food and water for the dogs, who were accustomed to returning there eventually though in some cases several days later, where their owners would find them.

The boy's dog was not included in these packs of foxhounds. For one thing the old hound was a solitary hunter by preference. And then he didn't bark on the trail so there was no way of even knowing if he was there or not. Also there were often fights between those dogs in the pack who were kenneled together and grew accustomed to one another, and any strange dogs put in with them, so the boy never asked that his dog be included. The men knew about the old hound, and they told the boy that he often joined in the hunt anyway. The next morning they would find him, footsore and tired, lying apart from the other dogs at the cages. Whenever anyone approached he would simply amble off and be swallowed up in the brush. Once or twice they reported that he appeared to be injured, presumably from a collision with a barbed wire fence or some obstacle in the dark, but the boy wondered if some of these wounds were from fights with other dogs. The old hound had lots of scars.

"What does he eat when he is gone for so long?" the boy once asked his father. "Whatever he can catch, or find," his father told him. Humpy Trundle assured the boy that the dog could catch deer, especially fawns in the spring and summer, and any animal that was weakened or starving during the cold winter months when there was snow on the hills and browse for the deer was scarce. "Folks what's seen your dog chasin' deer tell me he is a powerful runner," the old man told him. "And he didn't live this long bein' solitary but what he's also determined and resourceful. No, he can take care of hisself, I reckon," he told the boy. "Don't you worry none 'bout him. Your biggest worry is that one day he'll just wander off and not come back, same as he wandered in here in the first place." And the old hound did seem able to take care of himself. His wounds were never serious and they always healed; and although he would stay away for days and even weeks at a time he would return eventually and take up as if he had never been gone.

The boy never grew too close to the dog. He was fond of him, but it was more like an admiring—almost a grudging—respect, the kind you might feel for someone older and wiser. To the boy the dog was a symbol of a certain willfulness and independence, which he respected without completely understanding it or being comfortable with it. Even when they were alone together the boy sensed the gulf between them and he could see the vacant, disinterested look in the dog's eyes. He wondered what the dog thought and whether he cared for anything at all in the same way the boy did, the way the boy cared for the dog, or whether the dog was too wise for that. The boy considered the old hound wise in ways he hoped to be someday. Part of that wisdom, he knew, was in not trying to hold on too tightly to what was not really his, and not trying to change what was beyond his control. So when at the end of the third summer the dog disappeared one day and never returned, the boy was sad, but he didn't grieve. He knew that the dog had taught him something valuable. Life is a lot like that old dog, the boy thought.

And the man stood thinking about it again, as he watched the dog out the window and waited to see what it would do. In spite of the woman's coaxing the hound had not budged. It still stood motionless at the edge of the woods, regarding the woman warily. She continued to plead with it, holding the food extended in her outstretched hand.

She called to it again. "Come 'ere, boy. Come on now. Good boy." Finally the dog looked away as if to leave. "Come away from there," she yelled in frustration. At that the dog trotted into the woods and was swallowed up by the bracken and salal. When the man looked again there was no sign the dog had ever been there.

"Probably just a neighborhood dog," he tried to reassure her, "passing through from somewhere, on its way back home."

"I haven't ever seen that one before," she said. "I wish I could have run it off in the other direction."

"It would only come back," he answered.

The hound was following along the path taken by the fawn and the doe on those few occasions when they had seen them come out of the woods and into the yard. Unless they happened to spot the deer first and quieted their little dog, it would bark from within the house and the doe would instantly bound off with the fawn right behind. There was a trail there through the trees. He had been down it in one direction to where it circled back on itself in the thicket, and in the other direction to where it emerged at the edge of a pasture. The thicket was small, not more than two or three acres, and he was surprised that it offered the deer adequate cover or browse. With the completion that spring of another house, the thicket was bordered now on three sides by houses and yards and on the other side by an open pasture, beyond which there were other houses and a road. The nearest woods of any size was across the road, and even there the woods was broken up by more houses and farms for several miles before one reached the forest boundary.

There had been other deer in the yard but this doe was the only one that came regularly and he knew that it lived in the thicket. He had sat on the porch in early morning and late afternoon and heard it moving about in the underbrush; and periodically they would see it feeding in the bushes at the edge of the yard, or the little dog would catch its scent and utter low growls while staring intently at something they couldn't see but which he seemed to.

"Maybe it will have a fawn next spring," she said one morning. They watched the doe pick its way through the thinning cover at the edge of the clearing.

"It's only a yearling—too young for that," he told her. He didn't want to get her hopes up. He knew that soon enough it would become her deer. She would adopt it the way she did every wild creature. She had an affinity for anything wild. She was drawn to them and he guessed that in them she recognized something of that same impulse that stirred within her.

"What if it's only a small doe," she had suggested, "and not young after all. Why do you suppose it lives in our thicket?"

"To be near you," he had teased. "It's probably the yearling offspring of those other deer we saw in the yard," he told her. It was a small doe but he had no real notion of whether it was in fact a yearling. Since it was a doe, and by itself, he knew it could be older. "Besides, there are not likely to be any bucks around here," he said. "Not enough cover to satisfy them, I should think. They're more apt to stay in the big woods, where there are still plenty of clearings and burned areas for browse and more than enough females to occupy them. I'm afraid your deer has chosen a life of spinsterhood."

One of the things they both liked about this place was the forest nearby. The entire area had been logged eighty years ago, but since then it had grown up in Douglas fir and, on the wetter slopes, hemlock and cedar. At the edges of the clearings grew red alder. Along the creek beds huge big-leaf maples, covered with mosses and dangling licorice ferns from their branches, assumed grotesque, gargantuan poses. The forest itself was public land, but the edges of it were ringed with farms and clearings where deer and elk browsed in early morning and at dusk. Occasionally a black bear would wander out of the woods at night and turn over a garbage can, and once in broad daylight they had seen a huge bear lumber across the road, its shaggy coat rolling from side to side on thick layers of fat. An abundance of fresh water flowed into the sound nearby, and ducks and waterfowl of all kinds could be seen on the ponds and streams and in the salt water bays. In the fall and spring, salmon fought their way up the creeks where they spawned in shallow, gravelly pools barely deep enough to cover them with water before eventually dying. A profusion of plants and wildflowers grew in the warm wet climate and soon the woman had learned to identify most of them. On their walks she would point out shooting stars, candy flower, vanilla leaf, fairy lanterns, bleeding heart, purple nightshade, and the tiny delicate inside-out flower which was her favorite. They had chosen this place to live because it was not in a city; and although there were other families living close by, they were surrounded by farms and open countryside and the road to town wandered along the edge of the forest and through a picturesque valley. The thicket beside the house symbolized what had drawn them there.

Sometimes one or two of the bolder children in the neighborhood would venture a short distance into the thicket. It was grown up with blackberry vines around the edges, and with nettles and sword-fern and skunk cabbage deeper in, and in spring and summer the center of it became a mosquito-infested marsh so the children didn't play there often enough to disturb the deer. Dogs were the main threat. Every house had a dog and most of them ran loose at least part of the time. Now and then he would hear them barking in the thicket or at the edge of it, and he knew that occasionally they must be barking at the deer or their scent. Once or twice he heard excited barking that moved off rapidly in the distance, and he recognized that as a chase.

A single dog, especially a small one, did not pose much threat. Unless it were sick or injured a deer could easily outdistance a dog. One fall during hunting season he had watched as a buck and a doe stopped, unconcerned, to mate a scant few hundred yards ahead of a pack of beagles that were being used to keep the deer moving through the woods toward where the hunters were waiting. But most dogs would instinctively chase deer; and if they formed packs they could even catch one and kill it. He was surprised that the doe persisted in staying there and he knew that without luck a fawn would have little chance of survival.

Yet one morning there they were—the doe and a week-old fawn following at her heels and trying to nurse as she browsed. They emerged from the woods beside the house until both of them stood fully in the open, bathed in sunlight. The doe was nervous and never stopped but gradually moved away from the house toward where the trail entered the thicket on the far side of the yard. Every few seconds she raised her head abruptly to look around, fixing on something or some sound beyond the corner of the house. The large ears stood poised, erect. As she fed, the black-tipped tail swished from side to side, and periodically the doe raised one hind leg and kicked at the flies biting its heels. The fawn picked its way haltingly on spindly legs, keeping in the doe's tracks.

She had been the first to see them. "Come quick," she called. He knew at once what it must be and shut the little dog in the hall bathroom before joining her at the back door. "Oh, look," she whispered, "just look how pretty. How old do you think it is?"

"Only a few days, I would guess—a week at the most."

"So there was a buck," she teased.

"Must have been," he grinned.

"But you were right. She looks too small to have had that fawn."

"She's just a little doe. It's her fawn all right."

"It's still wobbly."

"That's just the jerky way it moves. It's too old to be truly wobbly."

"Can it run yet?" she asked.

"At that age they don't run," he said. "They lie motionless while the doe leads the danger away from them."

"Look at the dappled coat—like sunlight through the leaves."

When the fawn reached the wild daisies he had let grow up across the back of the lawn it stood momentarily camouflaged in a large field of white spots before moving out of sight into the woods.

They saw the doe and the fawn together in the yard a few more times after that. They came always in the morning, and on other mornings when they did not see them the little dog would stand at the back door and growl or give the short, snuffling snorts that meant he sensed something. After a while they stopped coming altogether and for three weeks they did not see them. Late in the afternoons he would still hear something moving about in the dense brush and detect the occasional snap of a broken branch or dead twig. He assured her they were still there although the longer she went without seeing them the more doubtful she grew. He always made a point of telling her whenever he heard sounds coming from the thicket, and she too would listen, but she never seemed to hear anything and she began to wonder whether he had heard anything either, or whether what he heard was only a squirrel or a towhee scratching in the leaves.

Then one evening near dark there was again a doe in the yard feeding on the yellow flowers atop the dandelion stalks. He called her to the window to see it. The two of them stood watching for a long time, but no fawn appeared.

"Is it even the same deer?" she asked finally.

"I can't be sure. The size is about right, but something seems different. A darker color perhaps? I don't know."

"It must be the same one. I wonder where the fawn is?"

"The coat seems grayer. And I believe this deer is larger."

"It's only the light that makes it look darker. Of course it is the same one." She sensed that he was being protective. "It's just that we don't want it to be. Something must have happened to the fawn."

"It could still be in the thicket, bedded down and hidden from view. Once I almost stepped on one."

"No," she said. "She's not nervous now the way she was before when the fawn was around. And she doesn't keep looking back toward the thicket anymore. I knew it couldn't survive. Too many people...and cars...and dogs. Like the birds and all the neighborhood cats. It's a wonder there are any birds at all...or any deer. I'm only glad I got to see it."

He knew she didn't mean it. From the moment she first saw the fawn she had wanted above all else for it to survive; to have it come out of the woods into the yard to eat the daisies and the dandelions and the ferns that grew there; to be able to stand unseen at the window and watch it, to see it lose its spots and grow up and become a big beautiful doe with a fawn of its own; and in that to look for a reassurance she found otherwise missing but for which she felt a longing; to know that everything after all is the same and that nothing ever really changes. "I was born a hundred years too late," she used to tell him, but then stopped after he began to challenge her whenever she said it. "How would you have known back then that you were happier than you could have been with all the things you have now, which the subsequent generations have lusted after and struggled and sacrificed to achieve; or that there might not have been some better, more golden age even earlier," he would ask her. He never pushed it too hard because at heart he felt the same way and it wasn't her that he was asking the question of but himself. In spite of the undeniable logic of the question he always concluded uneasily and somewhat angrily that she was right.

He knew also that in truth she did not despise cats. She had grown up with them and admired their independence and their idiosyncrasies. In the confrontation between the birds and the neighborhood cats she recognized the rightful claim of each and the nature of the fundamental conflict between them; but it was clear where her sympathies lay, if for no other reason than the birds were still wild and took all the risks, while the cats were domesticated and preyed on the birds without having to face even the prospect of an empty belly as the penalty for failure. Whenever she saw one of them stalking across the lawn toward the thicket she would slip out the door and head it off before it reached the spot in the salal where she knew a pair of towhees had nested that spring. She didn't know exactly where the nest was. Any attempt to locate it would only end up trampling down the vines and leave a trail that would alert predators to its existence. She had found nests before, some with eggs and some with nestlings, but whenever she visited them again to check on the progress of the occupants all she ever found were bits of broken eggshell or an empty, abandoned nest. She knew that most of them perished. She understood that and accepted it intellectually, yet emotionally birds were her special passion. She never went anywhere without a field guide and binoculars. Once she had held a tiny Brewer's sparrow caught in a banding net and pressed it against her ear to hear the rapidly beating heart and felt the warmth and vibrance that radiated from the fragile, pulsating life cradled in her hand. Oh, she uttered softly; and the magic of that moment was now a part of her, the feeling she had for that bird she had for all birds and all things wild. They flew free and mysteriously on their long migrations south in the fall and back north again in spring, and she yearned to go with them; to discover in the unfathomable mystery of something as simple and yet as complex as a feather, and creatures which by means of it and hollow bones and an enlarged sternum anchoring huge pectoral muscles fueled by a greatly increased metabolism could fly at all, let alone fly for seventy-two hours at a stretch, crossing two thousand miles of open water by night and day whether cloudy or clear, navigating by some means defying explanation but perhaps involving the stars and the sun and moon or the earth's magnetic field or some genetically programmed behavior itself as simple and yet as complex as a feather, but defying explanation nevertheless and likely to be still more mysterious and more wonderful even if eventually it could be explained in terms of something else which would then only have to be explained in terms of something else again—to discover in that unfathomable mystery the kind of reassurance which she found lacking in most other things but which she also found in the unexpected presence of the doe and its fawn in the thicket beside the house.

I should have lived on a farm, she told him; on that he never deigned to disagree. A farm constituted the maximum extent of civilization with which he could imagine her being comfortable. Everything beyond that had become for her, in its teeming excesses, the expression of ultimate absurdity—the towns and the cities, and now the uncontrollable urban sprawl spilling over into the surrounding areas to gradually absorb and coalesce them into one never-ending infrastructure of roads and shopping centers and dwellings—like some sort of voracious socio-amoeba ingesting and consuming everything in its path. She saw not its triumphs of the human spirit but its failures and its overriding preoccupation with whatever was trivial and frivolous. Not because of any tendency toward misanthropy—far from it. But because she was always on the side of the underdog; and because she believed in the rule of reason and in moderation as a principle embodying the instinctual wisdom of the ages; more important now by far than when the Hellenes inscribed on the temple at Delphi, "Know Thyself" and "Nothing to Excess", and then subsequently perished in its blind disregard.

"We can't help it," he told her; "it is part of our nature. Homo sapiens is a misnomer. Homo ministerium would be more accurate. We are by nature doers—managers—and out of that comes our irresistible urge to take charge and to change things to suit ourselves. If in the process we screw things up then we will fix that too, or so we believe. It is no one's fault, any more than being human is anyone's fault. We have behaved this way for as long as anyone is aware, and we will keep on until we accomplish whatever it is we are trying to accomplish—or perish in the process, which ultimately may be all that we are striving toward. Yet who could fail to be impressed with our successes? For that no great amount of intelligence is needed—merely curiosity and a sense of wonder—the same sense of wonder that should convince us how little we are capable of truly understanding but that instead we choose to interpret as proof of our special status. The twin admonitions of the Delphic Oracle were nothing more than some wiser head's expression of pessimism about the power of reason. No one listened then and no one is listening now. Each new success drowns out the voices of moderation in the excitement over some new bauble more bright and shining than the last, until by now no one remembers anymore why they wanted the bauble in the first place. The only thing we can be sure of is that it will continue until something beyond our control brings it to an end."

She understood that too and accepted it intellectually in the same way. But she didn't find any reassurance in it, the kind of reassurance she found instead in much simpler things, in things that were as they had always been, like the birds nesting in the thicket in spite of the predations of the neighborhood cats, or the doe and its fawn living where by all odds they shouldn't be. She retained a need for order and predictability in her life. It was that impulse that the old dog threatened when it turned and moved off silently into the protection of the thicket.

The rest of the morning she busied herself outside. That spring she had planted a small flower bed in a sunny spot at the edge of the woods, and for a while she pulled up weeds and watered the plants. The man went back to his work but occasionally interrupted what he was doing to return to the window and look out at her. Twice he caught her standing motionless, listening and staring at the thicket. Then she would go back down on her knees and continue to pick at the few green sprigs that still dotted the already clean, bare earth between the flowers.

Eventually, he thought, she will have to go in there and see for herself. To do that would risk disturbing the deer and perhaps call attention to the fawn if it were still there, and for that reason she had stayed out of the thicket until now. But the longer she went without seeing the fawn the more overpowering he knew the urge to explore the thicket would become. The surest sign she was thinking about it was that she never mentioned it to him. He would have tried to dissuade her, to shield her from the possibility of disappointment, and she knew that. So she said nothing. He understood just the same what she was thinking.

When she failed to stop for lunch he looked out again and found her poking about the edge of the clearing, looking under rocks to see what she would find and examining the low plants that grew among the vines and huckleberry bushes along the border of the thicket. While he watched she worked her way deeper into the underbrush, stooping now and then to crawl on hands and knees whenever something on the ground interested her. She might be looking for towhee nests or only following insects, but the real reason, he knew, was merely to find some pretext for being in the thicket.

The little dog stood at the screen door and alternately whined and issued the stifled snorts that signaled his interest in something deeper within the thicket. The man heard the sound of barking break out in the distance. He slid open the screen door and stepped out onto the porch to be able to hear better. The little dog stood attentively beside him, his pointed ears erect and directed toward the barking. Overhead, the sun shone down from a cloudless sky, as high above the horizon as it ever got in midsummer at these latitudes. There was not a breath of air stirring in the alders or in the aspen that rose in the distance over the center of the thicket, and the barking could be plainly heard. He could distinguish the sound of several small dogs he had heard before, and some that he didn't know.

Then among the cacophony of other sounds, he heard what he instantly knew was the deep throaty bellow of a hound. In the next instant the barking gave way to the snapping, snarling melee of dogs fighting, punctuated by frightened yelps and squeals of pain. Then more barking, and again he heard the hound.

Whatever is happening now, the chase is over, he thought, whenever he barks like that. Then more snarling and fighting, and the sound of some dog being severely punished by another.

"What is it?" she asked him. She ran toward where he stood on the porch.

"I'm not sure," he said, putting off giving her a direct answer. "Just some dogs fighting."

"But it's coming from the thicket." There was an urgency in her voice.

While he stood thinking of what to say next, suddenly from close by came the sounds of something crashing through the brush. He looked up in time to see two antlerless deer come bounding out of the woods in headlong flight. Their sleek summer coats glowed red in the sunlight. With two graceful leaps they crossed the far corner of the yard and lunged, crashing, back into the thicket where the trail re-entered it on the other side.

The dog beside him broke out in furious barking and streaked after the deer.

"C'mere!" he yelled.

"Stop him! Stop him!" the woman yelled and ran after the dog.

By the time she reached the other side of the yard the man had caught up with her but the little dog had disappeared, still barking, into the woods. The crashing of the deer through the thicket died out in the pandemonium of barking and yelling.

"Stay here!" he shouted. "I'll catch him. He won't get far," and he turned and dived into the salal and bracken. He headed straight toward the barking in front of him. The deer had followed the trail as the path of least resistance through the thick growth, and the dog was following the same way. Farther in where the undergrowth thinned he came to a dense growth of devilsclub crowding both sides of the narrow path, and there he found patches of deer hair hanging from the spiny thorns that grew on the thick stalks. Ahead he could see light through the trees where the trail emerged in a pasture and he knew he would catch up with the dog once he reached it. The barking in that direction had stopped. He could still hear the sounds of dogs fighting behind him. He had to hurry and get back. She would not remain idly by until he returned, and he didn't know what she might find at the site of the commotion.

When he reached the barbed wire fence at the edge of the pasture, he found the little dog standing and looking at him. He picked the dog up and tucked him under his arm and turned back toward the house. This time, familiar with the path, he hurried faster, running whenever the trail allowed and pushing blindly through the clinging devilsclub and blackberry vines with raised forearm to protect his face. When he broke out into the yard the woman was not there. Off to his left he heard dogs still barking, and mixed up with it now the sound of her voice yelling and pleading.

"Get away! Get away! Oh help me, please help," she sobbed.

Without waiting, he dashed toward the house to put the dog inside. He ran up the stairs and into the bedroom. He took from its place in the corner of the closet, a rifle, and from the shelf, a box of cartridges which he stuffed hurriedly into his pants pocket before running out again. He slammed the sliding glass door shut and fumbled for the cartridges in his pocket, spilling most of them on the porch while managing to stuff several into the tubular magazine, then chambered one and clicked on the safety.

He plunged into the thicket toward the sound of the woman's voice. He gave no thought to the trail now, taking the most direct route toward the noise. The swish of alder branches past his head and brushing against his clothes obscured all other sounds as he pushed forward. Every few yards he paused briefly to listen, then continued to fight his way through the underbrush toward her. He used the rifle held out in front of him to fend off the blackberry brambles and devilsclub that scratched his arms and tore at his clothes. Twice he stumbled over downed limbs and fell, and once a thick bough of thorns slashed a crimson row of scratches across the back of his hand when he turned and put out his arm to push through the tangled branches blocking his way.

The dry summer had left the normally marshy area in the center of the thicket passable and at last he reached the other side. In the dense shade the undergrowth thinned out and gave way to a low growth of ferns with cleared spaces in between. There on her knees in one of them was the woman, sobbing and lashing out in the midst of several dogs barking at her but keeping a respectable distance from the stick she wielded in one hand. Beside her on the ground he saw the spotted but torn and mutilated form of what he guessed could only be the fawn, and farther on, the body of a small dog whose fate at the fury of the hound he could readily imagine.

He saw that she was not hurt but only frightened and angry and frustrated. At her side lay the final, undeniable proof of what she had secretly feared from that first moment when she discovered the fawn in the yard and had to live afterwards with the constant thought of its precarious existence in the tiny thicket beside the house; and what she had dreaded but knew would come to pass the instant she spotted the solitary hound standing there at the edge of the yard and had watched helplessly as it moved off into the thicket, where she still dared to hope against hope that the fawn might, even then, somehow manage to survive. Now it was over, and she had lost; and the tears were only for what she had known would be the outcome anyway. More than with the hound or the worrisome dogs or what she knew was the inevitable fate of a deer trying to raise a fawn where the priorities of people and their activities took precedence, she was angry with herself; and with the hope which she had allowed to build beyond the realism that at core formed the one inviolable principle she always fell back on. They were simple tears of anger that burned her cheeks. She felt foolish and frustrated as she tried to fend off the dogs from the carcass of the fawn and thereby salvage some small measure of dignity.

"Stay away," she sobbed. "Oh please, make them stay away." She lunged forward on her knees at the dog nearest her which scampered back out of reach.

Normally they would have been a cowering bunch of mongrels, scurrying for cover at the first sign of the threat posed by the woman and the stick with which she swung at them. But they had tasted blood and the excitement of the kill, and now they were worked into such a frenzy that they were not individual dogs but a snarling pack, obeying the collective instincts of mob rule. What none of them would do alone, they dared together, barking and lunging and snapping at the woman, still trying to get at the fawn and rip it apart though it now lay dead and inanimate, the smell of blood fresh in their nostrils and driven by excitement and instinct to attack anything around them that moved.

He had seen it before, many times. Someone's pet which had never been out of the house or the backyard and which sat affectionately in your lap and licked your face would, if allowed to run free, form packs with other dogs and roam the woods and countryside killing deer and sheep or calves. He had come upon them and seen them slink away from a kill, unapproachable and wary together, then seen the same dog back home with its master, nuzzling someone's hand or letting some child pull its ears and twist its tail.

He had seen it with the foxhounds too. Dogs that individually would let themselves be petted and have their ears scratched would often become savage in packs, turning on and even killing each other in their fury. It was one of the first things he had detected in the eyes of the solitary old hound. A distant far away look that spoke of the unbridgeable gap separating the boy and the dog, a gulf across which each was willing and even able to reach part way but which both of them understood would always be there, standing between them. The hounds would kill the fox if they caught it. That they didn't very often was more to the credit of the fox than the hounds. The men and the dogs and the fox all understood that. The men were incensed if anyone killed a fox. For one thing it meant one less fox to chase; one less opportunity to sit in the dark and the deep quiet of the night and listen to the peculiar distant music of a pack of hounds pursuing a fox able to elude them at will and survive to run again and again. But if the hounds themselves killed occasionally the men accepted that. The boy knew too that the old dog was a killer—deer, certainly fawns, and whatever else he could catch, and foxes too, the boy thought, whenever he hunted with the other hounds. It was how the old dog had managed to survive and to remain independent, and the boy accepted that and would not have wanted it any other way, even when one day the old dog left and didn't come back. The little dog would behave the same way, the man knew. They are never completely tame, he thought; nothing is.

He saw her there, down on hands and knees, confronting them on their level and on their terms, with a stick wielded like a club to keep them at bay; from a kill rightfully theirs but which her own instincts demanded that she take possession of and shield from them. To them she was just some other animal and this just another conflict over possession of a kill. They were both back in the dim recesses of their distant pasts, obeying the same instincts they had always used to survive such confrontations. The hound had started it, he guessed; probably bringing down the fawn and killing it himself in their midst, then turning on the others when they tried to get in on the kill and refused to yield; killing one of them next and bloodying several more in the fight that ensued. Now the hound stood apart, off to one side, separate from the fray. Not threatening but once again solitary and aloof the way he had been that morning when the man watched him standing at the edge of the thicket looking back over his shoulder at the woman. His confrontation had been with the deer and the chase, and with the other dogs, not with the woman.

The man charged the lunging dogs. "Git!" he yelled, kicking at one small white mongrel as it ran past him. "Hi Yi! Git!" He plunged into their midst. This time the dogs scattered. They recognized in the man a new and different threat, and suddenly the spell was broken. It wasn't the rifle he held, or the fact that he had anything at all in his hands, that made the difference. It was what he represented, charging upright into their midst, yelling and threatening and taking control, that jolted them back and sent them scurrying. Only one or two stopped after that to bark a last time before turning and disappearing with the others into the undergrowth. He ran after them a few more steps to hasten them on their way, then came back and helped her, shaken, to her feet. In the confusion he had lost sight of the hound. When he looked around again he saw him, standing motionless off to one side in a little clearing in the ferns, farther away but still looking at them.

As he looked into the dark, implacable eyes he did not seem anymore to be seeing the dog in front of him, but past him, and past the present moment to the old hound and a time long ago, before that summer when he had simply trotted off into the woods and never come back; and he could see him plainly once more, the brindle coat and the bare patches of skin where no hair grew on the scars, and the empty, bottomless stare with which the old dog looked beyond him and on past to whatever it was lay on the other side of the gulf that stood between them, across which each of them had reached if only for a short while and only partially then; and he could still see the solitary hound looking at the boy who considered the dog wise in ways the boy hoped to be too someday and who had been wise enough even then not to try to hold on to what had not really been his; and then one day the dog had simply left and never returned, and it had been over.

As if he were still dreaming, he clicked off the safety on the rifle and put it to his shoulder. I'm sorry old boy, he thought, but I guess those days are over now.

She grabbed his arm. "No," she said quietly. "Don't." When he looked again the dog was gone.

THE EIGHTEENTH HOLE

The dog walked on ahead, slowly, snuffling at the ground as he went. He marked first the grass around a sprinkler head and then the edge of a patch of salal, following his nose steadily toward that special blend of musky earth smells and familiar scents to where he raised his tail and hunched his back to stand straining over the chosen spot. Afterwards he scratched at the thick fairway grass with all four paws, alternating one side and then the other, front and back feet, using the same motion the man had seen him adopt even as a puppy when he would raise one hind foot after another and paw comically at the air.

I wonder why they do it, he thought. He often wondered about it but he still didn't know. To cover over their scat, he had once surmised but soon came to doubt it. If that had at one time been the purpose it was seldom if ever achieved now in practice. Anyway, it seemed a curious, pointless reason. He had wondered too if it could be to clean their pads and prevent tracking feces to the den. That also seemed an unlikely cause. For one thing they didn't do it every time, and for another it contradicted the whole practice of scent marking by which they established territory. He didn't know if females did it too, but he didn't guess so. He had never seen one do it, but he had never owned a female so he just didn't know. He suspected the curious practice was a gesture of male dominance, like a fighting bull pawing at the ground or a male elk in rut. The little dog seemed more likely to do it whenever another dog was around, but not always then, and about equally whether the other dog was a female or a male. Maybe it was related to mating and was triggered by some particular scent. He had often watched the dog stand transfixed, its nose stuck in a clump of grass marked by another dog, until it drooled and slobbered on the ground and its lower jaw chattered uncontrollably, rooted to the spot by the chemical allure of some secret aroma. It was one of those mysteries he was never going to answer, at least not ever to his complete satisfaction. Still, he wondered about it.

The dog quit pawing the ground and continued down the fairway, stopping briefly to anoint each of its customary spots. By now the man knew them all. He took another sip from his cup of coffee and slung the remainder away from him and out across the grass, then held the cup turned upside down while the last brown drop of liquid ran down the inside wall. He stood for a moment and watched the narrow strip of newly wet grass steaming in the chill morning air. Then he slipped the cup into the pocket of his jacket and turned and walked up the broad fairway toward the dog.

Ahead of him in the slanted sunlight he could see a fine mist of spray from the sprinklers beside the eighteenth tee. Once there, he looked back unobstructed across a long reach of sloping ground to the flat surface of the eighteenth green nestled beside a single sand trap. Behind it and along both sides of the fairway stretched a dense screen of hemlock and Douglas fir, interspersed with an occasional cedar and carpeted with bracken and sword ferns. Bordering the grassy area to the right of the putting green was an asphalt road. There were houses beyond the green along both sides of the street, but they were set back in tall trees and were visible only from certain places. From here he could see none of them, and he had the feeling of being alone. That was why he came this way each morning. That and the fact the dog also preferred this route; not because of the privacy, for the little dog loved people, but simply because it was farther and he got to stay out longer. In the beginning the man had taken binoculars with him. But eventually he had identified all of the birds found here and learned to recognize them by their calls so that he no longer carried the binoculars.

This morning, as he stood looking back toward the shaded green, he noticed a dark figure strolling toward him through the shadows at the edge of the trees on the right side of the fairway. Whoever it was must have come from the street beside the green. There the conifers thinned out and gave way to a stand of alders and willows that formed an extension of the cultivated lawns. He had been looking in that direction the whole time he stood there, and he had seen no one until this figure startled him. It was tall and slender against the straight trunks of the trees. At first he had imagined a woman. But then he realized how tall she must be. An unaccustomed feeling came over him. Without thinking, he said out loud, "I wonder why that figure gives me the creeps?"

Though it was a long way off he was sure that the figure wore a black robe, covering the full length of its limbs, like a monk's habit only less bulky and hanging in loose supple folds. It could have been a sheer fabric like silk or rayon. A woman's silk pajamas, he thought to himself. Probably one of the neighbors, or perhaps a house guest accustomed to an early morning stroll.

When the figure looked his way it stopped, as though surprised it had been seen, and stood, regarding him. He didn't want to appear rude, or menacing, so despite his curiosity he looked away to where the dog was sniffing a clump of grass. He called to the dog in a low voice and began to move back in the direction he had come. After a few yards he paused and looked up again at the robed figure. It was moving slowly once more. Now that he was headed toward it, the dark form took a direction angling off into the trees.

He had time to study it at length. It moved with a smooth, fluid grace. He could make out what looked like white slippers and almost glove-white hands. But it was the head that caught his attention. It seemed too small, practically tiny, and though it was draped in a hood he could see what must have been a chalk-white face, unframed by any visible strand of hair. A sudden realization sent a cold chill through him. He stood riveted, never taking his eyes off the face. He could see it plainly now. The figure took one more step, looked toward him, then disappeared into the trees.

Calling to the dog, the man ran quickly to the spot where the figure had vanished. There were some paths through the trees, but even before he reached them he was certain he would find nothing when he got there. When he reached the street beyond, it too was empty. He stood looking up and down the street in the direction the figure would have taken, and then back along the paths in the woods. Nothing moved. Everything was still and quiet. Even the birds had stopped singing.

In the silence he became aware that his heart was racing from the slight exertion, and he felt suddenly light-headed. He took several deep breaths. His chest felt constricted, like someone had it in a vise and, little by little, they were tightening down on it and he couldn't quite get his breath. A dull persistent pain, by now familiar, crept around under his armpits and up to his shoulders.

He took another deep breath and sat down on the curb to rest. From his pocket he slipped a small bottle of white tablets and placed one under his tongue, then lowered his head between his legs. The little dog came over, nuzzled his face and stood patiently looking up at him. The dog seemed unsure what was wrong. He had not chased after the figure or given any indication that he had seen it. Now he looked at the man with a curious, puzzled cant to his head.

The man reached over and patted the dog's head. He was breathing easier now. He placed his fingers against the inside of his wrist and felt his pulse. He remained seated on the curb with his head lowered, waiting for the pain to subside. He could feel the gentle pulsing beneath his finger tips. The dog whined softly for a moment, then lay down beside him to wait.

THE BLACK HOUSE

At first they lived in a black house. It was a wood frame house made of the finest sawn cedar planks, but it was painted black. It sat far back off a curved street which was paved with asphalt and was also black, especially when it rained as it did often. The yard surrounding the house was thickly wooded with tall fir trees, and cedars, and it too was dark and gloomy.

The outside of the house was illuminated at night by lights shining upward from out of the thick salal and ferns that grew in the tangled undergrowth. Even so, the dark exterior of the house was not plainly visible but seemed to absorb the light which fell on it and to sink deeper into its surroundings.

It didn't really matter though. They were Scandinavian, or she was. Danish by birth, and she still spoke with the noticeably monotone accent derived from her native tongue. He was only Scandinavian by preference, having spent several years living there, learning the language and first marrying a Swedish woman from whom he had been divorced. He had subsequently improved his status in everyone's eyes by marrying Karen, for the Danes are a proud people and quite naturally hold themselves above their neighbors. Otherwise George was thoroughly American, though he had a decided preference, or rather a pretension bordering on affectation, for things European.

She was an appealing little thing, not tall, with a certain earthy glow about her. Her hair grew thick and straight and was bobbed under on the ends, pure platinum, just the way one might imagine a Danish woman. She was not actually beautiful, but attractive at least, even pretty, and probably best described as cute. She bounced when she walked. She walked each day around the neighborhood. By going twice around both main circles that were joined at one point through a short side street she could cover a total of three miles, which she did once in the morning and then again in the afternoon.

Most of the men in the neighborhood wanted to go to bed with her, or imagined they did. She looked like that. Like someone you would just naturally think of wanting to go to bed with. She had that kind of sexually wholesome appeal about her, not through anything she did overtly, but just by her presence and appearance.

None of them did go to bed with her however, although maybe a few of them did try. Because there was a sort of gloomy aspect about her too. Whenever one of them encountered her on her walks around the neighborhood and tried to engage her in conversation, she became nervous and distant. A kind of pall settled over her, made even more apparent by an unmistakable reticence and aloofness and by the evident agitation she exhibited at these exchanges. Those who tried to walk along with her and continue their conversations were soon discouraged by the tense, brittle laugh with which she punctuated everything she said, no matter how ordinary and insignificant. She gave no encouragement at all, no hint of any kind of warmth or interest. Still, they liked to look and think about what might be.

She had a beautiful daughter. The daughter was truly stunning and gorgeous. Tall, blond and statuesque, with full protruding breasts that stood upright where they were clearly discernible in the mind's eye beneath her blouse. She radiated the same healthy sexual glow that one noticed about her mother. All of the men in the neighborhood would have liked to go to bed with her, but of course none of them ever did, nor did they even try. That distinction, they each understood, would belong to someone younger with greater prospects, just as it should. Still, they did think about it and wonder what it might be like. The daughter's name is not important here. She eventually went off to college, then left home for good, and was, in time, more or less forgotten.

George was a professional engineer of some sort. He worked for one of the numerous state agencies, involved in energy policy—planning things. That's what George liked most. Being in charge and planning things, especially if the things being planned were never going to come about, like changes in the way we use energy. Nevertheless George was conscientious about what he did and gave the appearance of being quite serious. At parties, if you found yourself at a loss for something else to talk about, you could always mention some absurdity about this country's energy policy and George would gladly tell you how absurd things really were, how you couldn't begin to know the half of it, how things had to change soon, and so on, all offered with an air of supercilious superiority that set him apart as someone on the inside, someone in the know. But his stories really were comical, because, let's face it, most social policies, to say nothing of the situations they are intended to address, are absurd in a comical sort of way providing that you aren't personally caught up in them and aren't being inconvenienced all the time by what is actually happening. At any rate, George and his guests always had something to talk about.

There had even been a suggestion at one time among some in the neighborhood that perhaps the house was painted black to conserve energy, to make more efficient use of what little direct sunlight there was during the long, overcast winters, and to radiate heat more effectively for cooling at night in the summer. Those who knew the couple discounted that explanation. To them, black just seemed like a very natural choice.

George's work took him to Europe often. The European countries were far ahead of us in enlightened energy policy—that is, according to George—or at any rate, he said, in their thinking about such things. He went over on a regular basis to review what was being done to conserve dwindling energy resources for the future, and to collect crystal and Limoges and an occasional piece of art. The latest of these acquisitions were displayed prominently at their frequent dinner parties.

They liked to entertain. The only time Karen seemed at all comfortable around other men was when their wives were also present. Then she seemed merely indifferent, and spent all her time visiting with the wives. She was never completely at ease though.

For one thing, when George was not talking about his work he was apt to tell again the stories about how he had met and married Karen. He was living in Europe at the time, recently divorced from his Swedish wife and working for a U.S. firm. He got along well enough with the language but hadn't mastered the vagaries of certain slang expressions. When he was introduced to her parents, he referred to Karen by some term that he thought was an innocent expression of endearment but which actually meant that he was boinking her. They had all laughed uproariously at his mistake—that is, to hear George tell it—and afterwards he had fit right in. After all, they were very practical and open about sex, these Scandinavians, and George made it sound like there had been no problem. Karen also had been married before. The daughter was not George's and that is one reason, among others, why her name is not important.

One evening Karen dropped and shattered one of a set of very expensive cut crystal glasses while preparing to serve after-dinner liqueurs. George had brought them back from Europe the week before and this was the first opportunity to show them off to their guests. She became so distraught and nervous that in trying to pick up the pieces of the broken glass she managed to cut herself badly. George stalked out of the room in a barely controlled rage. He returned in a huff a little later and only made things worse by saying something unfeeling about how the set was ruined and by continuing to mutter under his breath various not-so-subtle slights. The guests shrugged it off and made the best of it, and everyone managed to get through the evening. That was just George's way, the wives told themselves. At any rate, that was the way he could be. I don't recall anyone in the neighborhood ever wanting to go to bed with George.

Afterwards they lived in a new house. It seemed everyone in California was suddenly moving into the area and paying what were outrageous prices for local real estate, but what were still, by California standards, incredible bargains. It became the thing to do: sell to the newcomers from California—who had more than likely sold a house there for several times what they were paying for a comparable or better one here—and then build a new, and bigger, house. So George sold the black house and built a new one in the same neighborhood.

This one was on a tiny lot from which all the trees had been cleared. All of the more desirable lots had long ago been sold and built on. The new house was an enormous monolith, spreading outward to fill the entire lot and stretching upward to loom high above the surroundings and the street below. The style was derivative of something Scandinavian. The cedar exterior was shapeless and bulky in outline, with few windows and an imposing two-story roof-line that enclosed high vaulted ceilings and vast volumes of unutilized internal space. Absolutely the worst possible design for energy utilization and efficiency. No sun penetrated the southern exposure, along which the three-car garage had perversely been placed to further insulate the rest of the house from any outside warmth. The front entryway hung suspended high above the ground, accessible by a wooden stairway spiraling upward two levels to a tiny porch nestled beneath a massive wooden door stuck midway up the front of the house. The cedar exterior was left natural, unpainted, and the whole structure looked like a gargantuan grotesquery of a mountain chalet, the kind one might expect to see perched high on the side of a hill deep in a spruce forest somewhere in the north country, except in this case plopped down here on a tiny, flat space cleared of all trees. At first appearance it seemed to be trying to sink its enormous bulk into the ground to reach some more reasonable level and become less conspicuous. Gone was the black, gloomy exterior of the old house. In its place stood the towering suggestion of something locked up tightly inside.

It had taken a long time to build the new house. There had apparently been problems with the builder and the subcontractors. No one was sure what the difficulty was. Whenever anyone encountered Karen on one of her walks and asked about it, she became even more nervous than usual and quickly changed the subject, or in the case of the men who imagined they wanted to go to bed with her, quickly hurried on her way. No one really wanted to talk to George about it. All anyone knew was that there had been problems.

Nevertheless, the house was finally finished and Karen and George and the daughter moved in. Or rather, they disappeared into it. About this time they stopped entertaining. On the rare occasions when there were guests for dinner, they were couples from outside the neighborhood that none of the neighbors knew. Most likely, the neighbors thought, they were people with whom George was associated at work.

After George had planted grass and a few shrubs and flowers and had the yard generally arranged the way he wanted it, he was seldom seen outside. On occasion the garage door would be open and a car would be seen coming or going, but other than that the house stayed closed up. The few windows were all high above the ground where no one could see into or out of them. Even those who passed by at night on their walks about the neighborhood could see no shadows against the dimly lit vaulted ceilings onto which the windows peered. Whole weekends would pass with no signs of life coming from the house.

For a period Karen stopped taking her customary walks. About that time George began doing a lot more traveling in his job. He was gone for long stretches at a time. The daughter went off to college and was seldom seen anymore, not even in summer when school was out. At some point she was gone for good. No one knew exactly when or where. There was no indication or mention of a wedding and no notice of one in the local newspaper.

George would be back for brief periods, then he would be off to somewhere else. Gradually Karen resumed her daily walks, always with the same nervous agitation whenever she encountered any of the men in the neighborhood. Sometimes she was seen walking with a woman that no one knew.

Finally, George retired from his job. He had been very successful financially, with investments he made in energy companies, and he retired early I found out later. Not long after that, he died. He did not have a happy death, but died in a rage, I was told. I am not surprised, and I am even a little reassured and glad of that, considering how one has to live. The man who bought the black house never changed its color. When it was time to repaint it, he painted it black again. When asked why, he said that it would be impossible to ever cover up such a dark color completely. No matter how one tried the black would always bleed through. For years afterwards Karen could be seen walking around the neighborhood, once every morning and again in the afternoon. She never lost the tense, brittle laugh which punctuated her conversations with whatever men tried to talk to her during her twice-daily walks. The new house remained closed up tightly.

THE CAMPAIGN

It was late summer, August, and the campaign signs for the fall elections had started showing up around the county. Soon, like the mushrooms that appeared after every rain, signs and placards bearing the names of candidates and the offices they were campaigning for began to spring up everywhere. They were posted along every well-traveled route in the county, nailed to fence posts and stuck upright into the soft ground of the cleared ditch banks beside the road. They sprouted in the lawns of ardent supporters, and appeared like weeds in little clusters in the fields of those farmers who would grant permission or who were simply too busy with other matters to remove the ones placed there without bothering to ask permission. Whether the hopeful portents of some future promise, or merely the lingering markers of an unfulfilled legacy, those who saw them and paid little notice seldom bothered to ask.

Sue Billings knew she had to get busy. Sue was a candidate for county assessor, and she wanted to allow two full months for her campaign before the elections on the first Tuesday in November. This would be her second campaign. She had been county assessor now for one and a half terms.

Sue came from a political family. For three decades her father had directed the fortunes of the Democratic Party in county and local politics. Three years ago at his request, the Governor had appointed Sue to head the assessor's office after the incumbent died suddenly of a heart attack in midterm. Not that Sue had any political ambitions of her own. Not at the outset anyway. She had taken the job to advance her husband's career. Jeff was a lawyer and a member of the state legislature and they both knew the advantages of incumbency and political favors and the right connections.

Jeff was young and ambitious and had aspirations for higher

office. Although they had a good marriage in their own right, her father's political connections had not been lost on Jeff when he was courting Sue. Even back then he had begun to think in terms of being Governor someday, or maybe U.S. Senator, and he had dropped hints to that effect whenever he and Sue's father talked politics. The older man recognized in Jeff those attributes that made such ambition a realistic one, and had not only encouraged him but had cultivated and groomed Jeff for what both of them had come to hope would be a bright and successful political career.

County assessor was a fairly safe position. Incumbency and affiliation with the right political party were enough to assure tenure. It was not a very demanding job. It required some rudimentary managerial skills, an elementary knowledge of accounting and record-keeping, and the common sense necessary to deal with the public and handle routine personnel matters. Sue possessed all of these; in fact, she excelled at all of them.

The previous county assessor had held the position for a record ten terms, and had left his stamp on both the office and the staff. When Sue took over she found in place a smoothly functioning bureaucracy. The records were well organized and documented. Even though everything was done by hand, tax notices were mailed out on time and delinquencies were promptly followed up. The clerical staff understood how the system worked and could function with a minimum of supervision; in truth, with no real supervision at all other than that imposed by the careful organization of the job, itself the culmination of years of trial and error.

To her credit, Sue made no changes when she took office. She kept a very low profile, allowing the existing staff a free hand at carrying on business as usual while she learned from them how the office operated. She made certain that no one felt threatened by her presence, and occupied herself with learning the system already in place.

She worked hard at it, arriving before anyone else in the morning and staying late into the evening. Before long she had mastered even the finer points of the procedures and was asking questions which indicated to everyone in the office that she was clearly on top of her job. Even so, she interfered as little as possible with the daily routine. She continued to rely on the judgment of the staff in all matters but those which they brought specifically to her attention. In a few months Sue had gained the respect and admiration of the old-timers, who then began to do what every good bureaucrat must rely on in order to survive: they conducted their affairs with an eye to protecting her, as the one who would have to bear ultimate responsibility for any mistakes. Word went out that this was a very savvy lady, and Sue ran for re-election at the end of her first year in office.

As predicted, she won, against someone even less well known than she was. Not by a large margin, but by an amount substantial enough to satisfy the party regulars. The pundits had projected the winning margin at the beginning of the campaign, before Sue ever canvassed her first neighborhood or shook her first hand. In fact, they advised her against a vigorous campaign. As the incumbent she had the advantage. The Democrats were strong in this county, and always had been, and all she had to do was avoid making any outright blunders. Since she couldn't point to any particular accomplishment of her own, beyond the good judgment not to screw-up an already well-functioning operation, Sue simply went through the motions and let the campaign take its course to a narrow, but satisfying, victory.

Privately however, Sue knew that she had done a good job in her first year. Her success had awakened in her an ambition she had not known was there before. She wanted to do more than be a figurehead, someone content to go through the motions, living off the accomplishments of what her predecessor had worked hard for twenty-one years to build and which the existing staff could continue to implement without her help for many more years to come. She wanted to achieve something on her own. Still, when Sue looked critically at the job she realized that restructuring it merely for the purpose of leaving her own stamp on it made little sense. She had to admit that the procedures in place worked well just the way they were. The staff would only resent any unwarranted attempts to change things just for the sake of change, and would be put off by it. No, instead she would leave everything pretty much the way it was. She would look for some other way to make her mark.

It was then that Sue Billings began to think about what it meant to be charged with the public trust, about the solemn duty of being a public servant. The notion of serving the public interest took shape in Sue's mind as an ideal which transcended personal ambition and partisan politics. She began to think of herself as one entrusted with a grave responsibility. She gave no thought to the long hours she worked, for what was, after all, a very modest salary. She had no need of the money. Her family was well-to-do, and Sue was the sole heir. She didn't think of it as a job at all. She was an elected official, chosen freely by ballot in what was the most sacred ritual of representative government. And she had been entrusted to protect and promote the public good. This became her single ambition and the guiding principle that shaped her actions.

As her first goal she set about to make the operation of the county assessor's office even more effective and efficient. The major impediment was that everything had to be done by hand. She lobbied for and obtained funds from the legislature to purchase needed computer equipment. The tax records were entered into an electronic data base for easier access and updating. Software routines which made it possible to interrogate the files stored in the computer were acquired and implemented. Soon all tax notices were being processed and printed by computer, reducing to just a few weeks a task that had once taken the staff several months to complete. Now it was possible to follow up each delinquency in more detail, mailing additional notices and searching the records for the correct addresses of current property owners.

As a result, tax revenues for the county increased, and owners who might otherwise have lost their property at auction for tax delinquencies were tracked down and notified in time. All the while the work became easier, more enjoyable. Clerical errors decreased and worker morale improved. Sick leave and absenteeism among the staff declined. People volunteered to work overtime without pay during periods of peak activity. Letters from appreciative taxpayers arrived in the mail and were posted for all to see and take pride in.

Efficiency improved, yet no jobs were lost. The new methods made it possible for the same staff to accomplish more work. Now there was time to reassess all of the current property valuations, bringing them into line with present market values. The result was a dramatic burgeoning in tax revenues available to the county and the state. The increased revenues meant that new taxes did not have to be proposed, and several bond issues were set aside. The county commissioners and the legislative oversight committee on budget revenues took notice and sent commendations to Sue and her staff. Even the Governor visited and offered his congratulations.

At the end of her first full term in office Sue Billings had a record of solid accomplishments that she could point to with pride, and she was looking forward to running for re-election on the substantial merits of her own record.

It promised to be a challenging election. Her opponent was a young and energetic accountant with a wholesome, attractive wife and two small children, who was active in church and civic affairs—altogether an appealing candidate. The Republican Party, sensing a taxpayers' revolt as a result of increased property valuations, was backing his candidacy with all of their resources.

One evening at a party Jeff introduced Sue to someone he said could help plan her campaign. He was one of those public relations specialists with degrees in psychology and communications, and a proven track record of managing successful political campaigns. He had managed the Governor's last campaign.

"How much do you have to spend?" he asked her. "Well, not a lot," she said; but then she outlined for him her accomplishments and the strategy she envisioned for getting her story across to the voters. "No," he said, "I think that's the wrong approach," after Sue finished telling him about herself and her opponent. "Too risky. You are up against what your opponent symbolizes to the voters. Tell you what," he said, "let me think about it. Give me a few days and I'll come up with a proposal for something that will work better."

"Listen to him," Jeff told her. "He knows what he is doing. He usually gets big bucks for managing a campaign but in this case he is going to do it as a personal favor. The law firm is representing an important client of his."

"It can't hurt anything to hear what he has to say," Sue's father told her.

So she met with him a week later, still thinking of ways to present her story to the voters and hoping to get from him ideas to that end. Instead, he had set up in his office an easel on which was mounted a single piece of large white poster board, covered over by a sheet of thin white tissue paper.

"You want to keep it simple," he told her. "I have here an idea that I think will work." He had not really listened to anything Sue had been telling him. He turned back the sheet of paper covering the poster board and revealed a simple, but elegant and beautiful design. The colors were the thing. They were vivid and indelible, stunning and hypnotic. Once glimpsed, they captured and held the gaze of the viewer. Afterwards they could not be gotten out of mind.

In the center of the poster stood a large, brilliant fuchsia oval shaped like one of those old ornate frames that hold the photographs of elegant women. The fuchsia oval lay on a shimmering emerald background, like the petal of a beautiful, delicate flower against a luminous green leaf. The emerald background was shaped like two truncated pyramids placed base to base, and the whole thing called at once to mind an elegantly simple watch face with a brilliant fuchsia crystal. The shape of it suggested a certain timeliness, but also a vast and eternal timelessness. The image was captivating, and at the same time soothing and reassuring. Printed on the upright oval, in simple, unadorned black letters outlined in white, was the word Billings; and below, in smaller letters, Assessor. That was all.

When he uncovered it, he said nothing. Sue stood there staring at the poster, unable to take her eyes off of it. She wanted to voice an objection. "You mean that's it, that's all, the whole campaign is to be this one poster?" But she didn't, she couldn't. The figure kept drawing her back.

When she tried to look away after staring at it for a long interval, she discovered a startling and curious effect. The image appeared before her eyes once more, now against the white wall where her gaze came to rest, this time with the colors reversed, but with the outline of the words still visible against the now green oval on the fuchsia background. No matter where she glanced the image remained before her eyes.

"I don't understand," she said.

"It's a simple optical effect," he started to explain. "But why isn't really important. It's only one of the subtleties of this approach. I have surveyed the campaign signs seen around here. Most of them are drab and unimaginative, like the people they represent. They are cheaply printed, black on white, and the lettering is too small and cramped to be clearly visible; or they try to say more than can be quickly read and retained.

This one is different. It is an image. A work of art. A friend of mine who is an abstract artist created it for me. If you do not adopt it, he will likely frame it and hang it in his next show. However, he likes causes and has agreed to help us. Success, and the affirmation of his art, is all that he seeks in return. Everything about the image is important: the colors, its shape, the proportions of the figure, they must all be preserved. Placed before the voters it will come to represent you. And on election day, in the privacy of the voting booth, your image—and your name—will be the one that surfaces."

"But the record," Sue protested. She wanted to talk about her accomplishments, her vision for the future, she said.

"You may do so if you wish," he told her, "but I advise against it. Symbols are less confusing and more reassuring than the dull facts of our existence."

During the next two months Sue spent every spare moment

talking to voters. After work and on weekends she went from house to house, knocked on doors, stood on street corners and frequented shopping malls. There was time enough to contact only a small fraction of those who could vote and Sue felt a growing sense of urgency. Yet everywhere the response was the same. "Oh yes, I have seen your poster," each of them said. She talked about her service to the public. "How did you ever think of it," they wanted to know? She ticked off the milestones of her record during the past two years. "When I close my eyes I can see it still," one told her. "What does it mean," another asked? Sue mentioned her plans for the future. Most were polite, but they wanted to talk instead about the poster. They did not want to discuss Sue or her record. They felt they already knew her. At every turn they greeted her and shook her hand and asked her about the poster.

Sue won the election by a landslide. It was the largest margin of victory anyone could recall. Following the election her staff threw a victory celebration, with cake and champagne. They presented her with a campaign poster, matted in a fuchsia border and mounted in a large plain gilt frame. They insisted she hang it in a prominent place above her desk.

The fuchsia oval on the green background was adopted as the official department logo. It was featured on the office letterhead. The artist was awarded a copyright on the use of the image. Soon forgotten were the legislative commendations and the letters of appreciation from the Governor. Overlooked were the statistics and tax revenues that measured the performance of the assessor's office. Long after the other campaign signs and placards had faded and wilted and decayed back into the earth from which they had sprung along roadsides and in fields and lawns, still could be seen here and there, tacked to an occasional fencepost or plastered on some abandoned billboard, the memorable white poster bearing the strangely indelible image.

Whenever Sue Billings tried to bring up her accomplishments as county assessor, the conversation invariably turned to the subject of the poster.

THE BOXING LESSON

The other boy just stood there, swaying from side to side and staring straight ahead, still poised, as if not fully aware that the pummeling had stopped. A thin trickle of blood flowed from each nostril into the corners of his mouth and ran in bright rivulets down the sides of his chin to drip onto the front of his shirt. His hair lay plastered in wet ringlets and his face glistened with sweat and thin splotches of crimson where the blood-smeared gloves had landed.

"What in God's name do you think you are doing?" the woman screamed. The others had run to get her when the fight started to get out of hand.

"Mrs. Johnston, Mrs. Johnston," they yelled, "come quick! Bobby's nose is bleeding—bad!" She had followed after them, running as fast as she could all the way from the trim white house across the broad green yard that stretched toward the open fields beyond, and out behind the gray weathered barn where the two boys stood facing each other at arms length, the one with his nose bloodied and his gloves still raised, his face an expressionless mask.

The taller of the two boys stood immobile, passive now, hands by his side, unheeding, and eyed the other boy, trying to sort through the tangle of his own emotions. He slowly became aware that the woman was screaming at him, and then he realized that she had been for some time, that everything else had grown quiet, the others standing around watching the two of them and the woman to see what would happen next.

Andy glanced at the battered figure across from him and saw a look of sullen defiance return to his face. The smaller boy took no notice of the woman's presence but stared straight back at Andy, ignoring the bleeding nose and sweat-filled eyes. He kept his arms raised, gloves in front of his face, to ward off the blows that had repeatedly and unerringly found their mark. Nothing in his expression betrayed any expectation of leniency, nor any willingness to entreat for it or accept it.

Jesus, he can take a beating, Andy thought to himself. The realization brought a disturbing apprehension. He glanced around nervously to assure himself he had not uttered it aloud. The blood-smeared face and shirt of the other boy elicited his admiration and made him uncomfortable. Under each of the boy's eyes Andy could see a puffy welt beginning to form. His own face was largely unmarked. Most of the blows he had taken were glancing ones off the sides of his own gloves, and lacked the sting to do any real damage. He was bigger and quicker than his opponent, with longer arms and more experience. But the other boy had withstood his best punches without a whimper, never once showing any sign of quitting, until the woman's screams had intruded and stopped it. Even now the boy just stood there, calm but defiant, with the blood trickling down his face. Andy felt confused and ashamed.

"What in God's name are you doing?" the woman screamed again. This time Andy knew she was speaking to him.

"I was teaching him to box," he said. Even as he said it he knew it sounded like an alibi. He looked around at the others, who averted their eyes or stared at the ground, embarrassed at having been found out. Most of them had been yelling and cheering just moments before. They were embarrassed for themselves, but also for Andy. For what could be seen as a mismatch in the bloodied and bruised face of the other boy who had endured blow after blow to remain standing at the end, his battered face attesting to the unevenness of the contest even as his still defiant form held the final outcome hostage.

The woman started toward the other boy. Andy quickly stepped forward and placed a hand on the boy's shoulder.

"Are you all right?" he said.

The boy turned away, taking a swipe at his bleeding nose with the back of a gloved hand. For the first time there were tears brimming in the corners of his eyes. Andy knew they were not from pain but were tears of anger and humiliation. The boy's shoulders shook as he began to sob. Andy put his arm around him.

"I'm sorry," he said. "I'm really sorry. I didn't mean to hurt you."

The other boy was unable any longer to hold back the shame and frustration that each of the unanswered blows had made him feel. In his humiliation he tried to wipe away the streaming tears with the blood-smeared gloves until his face took on the rouged look of a sad-faced circus clown. Andy searched for something else to say. He knew there was nothing he could do to assuage the hurt.

"I'm sorry," he said. "I'm sorry."

The woman kneeled in front of the sobbing boy. She lifted the front of his sweat-soaked shirt and wiped the blood from his mouth and nose. Then she dried his tears, pulled him tight against her and held him fast for several moments. The slender form shook all over with convulsive sobs. The other children began to drift away, hoping to escape notice. When the woman released the boy, his mouth and nose were again bloody and she once more wiped his face and eyes with the tail of his shirt.

"Come along, Bobby. We have to get that nosebleed stopped," the woman said. She led the sobbing boy in the direction of the house. Her clear blue eyes turned back, and for a moment they met Andy's with a familiar look of quiet sadness. Then she turned away and he was left standing there all alone.

Andy had taught himself to box, from books and by reading the accounts of professional fights in the magazines he sometimes found in the barbershop. He listened each Saturday night to the fights on the radio, lying alone in his room in the dark, picturing in his mind what he had read in the books and in the magazines as the voice on the radio sketched the actions of the fighters. He learned all about how to lead with a left jab, holding his right hand ready in reserve; and about watching the other fighter's eyes and head for clues that he was about to jab, timing his own punches to beat him by just enough to spoil his rhythm and make him miss, so that the arm with the heavy glove would snap fully extended and cause pain in the elbow. Learning that right-handed fighters sometimes drop the right hand when they throw a left jab, and when that happens you can come across it with a stinging left to the head, followed by a hard right. Learning to keep his own head moving to make it a more difficult target; and to keep the body moving at the same time, circling to the right against a right-handed boxer and away from his right hand, or to the left against a southpaw. Learning to constantly circle while he punched which was the most difficult of all since it required coordination and concentration to land punches from a moving stance. Discovering that a southpaw is the most dangerous to fight, since his jab comes at you from the side with which you lead, while his stance takes his head and body farther from the reach of your own right hand. And one learned always to jab first against a southpaw, to keep his right hand out of your face, watching for any tendency he had to drop the left when jabbing; countering when that happened with a right thrown with the arm and shoulder carried high to protect the head from the lowered left hand, trading at most a punch to the body for one that could end the fight. And if nothing else worked you had to take chances against a southpaw, by getting inside where you could use the right hand, parrying the jab away with the left while stepping forward to throw a fast, hard right whose speed and accuracy were everything because if you hesitated or missed you were walking straight into the good left hand of your opponent and leaving yourself open at the same time. Learning to cover up at times against any kind of fighter, holding the elbows in close against the body with the arms vertical in front of the chest, gloves in front of the face, so that you could only be hit by glancing blows from the other fighter's gloves. Learning that to win you first had to survive and that could only be assured by not getting hit. All these things he had learned and rehearsed over and over in his mind, practicing them against any boy in the neighborhood he could entice into putting on the gloves.

Andy mowed lawns for most of a summer to earn money for the gloves, twelve-ounce ones made of leather, dyed red. Their weight made them too heavy and cumbersome for Andy to throw a punch hard enough to really hurt anyone, beyond an occasional bloody nose or swollen eye. He discovered that most of his opponents could not tolerate being hit on the end of the nose, or having their nose bleed, and these he could beat easily by flicking repeated jabs to the face.

He practiced everything he learned until it became not just something he knew from reading a book, but until it was second nature and he could use it without thinking. Andy felt the pride of accomplishment in what he could do and in the knowledge that he could do it well. As he refined his skills he began to teach some of the others what he had taught himself. Most of them he turned into better opponents, more adept at defending themselves. But none of them acquired Andy's passion for boxing, or his desire, and they fought only because he cajoled them into it with whatever argument or inducement proved effective. In the end it always ended up seeming too easy for him. No matter how he tried Andy couldn't escape a nagging doubt that undermined his confidence.

It was the same feeling he would encounter later whenever he shot at a sitting bird, or when the ducks were landing in the decoys and he timed his shots as they were flaring out to settle onto the water rather than taking them on the wing overhead. Or when the shooting was easy and he took too many doves or quail, or more than his fair share of the shots; or when he killed a turkey whose beard, or a spike buck whose antlers, made legality a fine point of contention. In each instance the feeling of success was sullied by an insinuation of something undeserved and dishonest. Then, just as now, he felt diminished and ashamed.

This opponent had learned well, better than any of the others. In spite of that he was still no match for Andy. He lacked Andy's desire and without that he was overmatched because he gave away an advantage in both size and speed. Yet he was a good defensive fighter and he never quit. Plus, he was a southpaw.

Andy convinced the boy to spar under the guise of taking it easy and giving him a boxing lesson as they went along, allowing him to practice jabbing and parrying jabs at which the other boy excelled. It had started out that way. Then at some point Andy let his right hand drop during a series of light jabs and the other boy caught him by surprise with a solid left hook, sending the beads of sweat flying from Andy's head; then startled him with two more quick jabs and hit him with another left before Andy could regain his composure. Andy moved away and managed a congratulatory comment; but he was chagrined and angered by the momentary lapse and the adrenalin had started to flow.

From that point the nature of the contest shifted to one in which Andy displayed his own skills; taking advantage of every weakness he could discover in his opponent's technique, moving all around him, throwing flurries of jabs in quick succession, followed by rights each time he found an opening, counter-punching whenever the other boy attempted to put together combinations, scoring on every exchange until he was swept up in the euphoria of total mastery. Andy ceased to regard the other boy as a person he was boxing, but as something to be dominated and conquered, against which he could affirm his superiority and reassure his shaken confidence; not thinking about what he was doing, just reacting to the explosive compulsion of ego.

For a while the other boy held his own, taking confidence from the punches he knew had shaken Andy, believing in himself for a brief instant. But the blows fell too relentlessly and finally his confidence betrayed him. Under the onslaught he reverted to protecting himself, unable to put together punches that didn't leave him open to further punishment. Even then he refused to just cover up, but continued to move and to jab, covering up only whenever the blows came too fast and too hard.

Soon he was hurt, unable to make the fight any sort of contest. It quickly turned into something which neither the boy nor those watching wished to see continue. But Andy was relentless, shutting out everything except the feeling that came from being able to dominate his opponent. He used everything he had taught himself until the other boy was a punching bag reduced to covering up under the rain of blows, still refusing to quit. Then the woman's screams brought him back to the reality of what was happening and the blood-splattered face looking back at him reduced him to feeling small and confused and ashamed.

Andy watched as the woman led the boy sobbing toward the house. The others drifted away without speaking, leaving him standing there by himself. Deep inside he knew the feeling of disgust and a strange kind of loneliness.

He can really take a beating, Andy thought again. His admiration was deep-felt and genuine. I hit him with everything I had and he stood there and took it and never once quit. Andy wished now it had been the other way around. He felt strangely isolated and unsure of himself. He remembered the boy's sobs, and the look of sadness in the woman's eyes. He stood there all alone and began to feel cold in the slight breeze.

THE STREAK

At the opening tip-off Brad outleaped the other center and flipped the ball over the head of the opposing guard. In unison the Kid broke around his man, took the ball off the floor on the first bounce with his right hand and dribbled down the court. Instead of driving toward the basket he faded left into the corner, unguarded, and put up a long, lazy jump-shot with no one near.

During the pre-game warm-ups he had hit ten in a row from that same spot and he thought he might as well find out early how it was going to go.

The ball followed the flat low-arching trajectory that had become his trademark. "Son," the coach yelled in practice, "you don't have any touch on your shot. Shoot the ball up higher—put some arch on it. Those rifle shots ricochet off the rim. Cuts down on any chance for a follow-up."

Cody had grown accustomed to Coach's comments. He knew too that Coach was right. Cody understood the mental aspect of the game, how to play the percentages, the soft, deft touch on the ball that converted near misses to shots which hovered around the rim and eventually dropped through for points. But he was strictly a streak shooter. When he was on with his shot there was no need for any follow-up. And tonight, warming up, he had felt a streak coming on.

They were real crowd pleasers too, those flat jump-shots of his. The ball wasted no time getting there, seeming to just clear the front of the rim before ripping the net sideways as it dropped through. He watched as this one deflected sharply downward off the back of the rim and appeared to go right through the center of the net without slowing down. The crowd erupted, and the noise with its strangely soothing effect washed over him.

For an instant he remained poised, transfixed, frozen in time and place, experiencing the shot again, picturing it in his mind and feeling it in his muscles, the entire sequence captured in one simultaneous sensation of sight and sound and feeling. The rim loomed enormous in front of him, the ball passing easily through it, right off the tips of his outstretched fingers as he hung suspended, wrapped in the roar of the crowd, watching it go through, capturing the image in his mind and the feeling in his muscles to call them up again and again, shot after shot, each time the image and the feeling exactly the same while the streak remained alive.

This one was for all the marbles. The winners would be the new state champions, and the losers—well, the losers could try again next year or go through life thinking about what might have been. For his part, he didn't want to spend any more time worrying about what might have been.

At the other end of the court he played a loose zone defense, keeping well off his man and giving him lots of room. These two teams had met twice before. He knew the guard on the other side of the court had a tendency to get careless and sloppy with his cross-court passes when the defense didn't press.

He saw it coming. He stepped quickly in front of the ball, picked it off, and headed back down the court for the basket. He didn't have great speed—good hands, but not enough speed to cleanly win a footrace to the basket—so rather than get hacked on the lay-up he pulled up short at the top of the key and hit another flat jumper that looked as if the ball were drawn to the hoop and sucked through it by some giant invisible force.

Half of the crowd was now on its feet. The noise had swollen to a sustained, steady roar, smooth and soothing, which he did not hear in any way he was actually conscious of, but sensed instead, pressing against his skin as it flooded over him and drew him into its protecting isolation.

"Yeah!" he muttered to himself. He had the image fixed clearly, indelibly in his mind, felt the shot in every fiber. He was conscious of nothing but the mental image and the feeling of the ball going through the hoop, as the swelling surge of the noise and his own unremitting rhythm insulated him from everything else.

He was on automatic now. He had the sensation of being able to summon up that image and that feeling on demand, to hold it in his mind and his muscles as a template to guide the ball on the next shot, of being able to will the ball through the hoop anytime he wanted. He had always been able to concentrate best in such situations. Immersed in the noise he shut out all awareness of the crowd. They were there not as individuals but as a general indistinct blur, as an amorphous thing somehow associated with the noise but held at bay by it. There was an irrevocable flow to the events on the floor. He became swept up in it, conscious not only of what was happening immediately around him but of what was happening everywhere on the court, aware of it all simultaneously and responding to it automatically, not having to think but merely reacting, playing the game the way he had learned it, the way the game itself dictated that it be played. He moved in unison with the flow; moved with it and directed it.

"Defense now! Defense!" The shouts came from the bench as they moved back up the court. This time they came out of their zone and pressed, and finally, unable to penetrate, one of the forwards on the other team took an outside shot in frustration and missed. Brad swept the ball off the backboard and fired a quick outlet pass which Cody took on the run. The flow surged past him and he slowed the pace.

As point guard he ran the plays, which consisted of moving the ball around, trying to find the open man. They were a scrappy bunch of opportunists, nothing fancy or sophisticated, just waiting for the other side to make a mistake, to fall back even only one step and leave an opening. He passed the ball to Theo in the near corner, who was immediately cut off and passed it back; then over to Gil, the other guard; from Gil the ball went to Ontoveros in the far corner, back out to Gil, in to Brad who was playing too high on the post for any kind of shot, then back out to Cody, over to Gil again who passed it in to Brad now on the opposite side of the lane. Well, if no one else was going to shoot, Cody thought, then he would. Taking advantage of the screen set by Theo, he took the pass from Brad in the corner and put up his third straight jump shot, this one touching nothing but net.

Yeah! he exulted. Oh Yeah! Yeah! Yeah! Waves of exhilaration rippled through him. It felt as if every nerve in his body fired in unison, sending dizzying bursts of elation sweeping over him.

This was what he played the game for, those times when it all came together and everything worked. Those moments when nothing else mattered, not the long hours of practice, not the pain and the physical fatigue and the sacrifice, not the defeats, nothing but this one magical moment, this reassuring feeling of well-being and elation. At such moments he could believe in the future, in the triumph of right over wrong, that somehow all of this made sense and that everything would work out for the best.

On their next possession Las Cruces scored and the crowd quieted. The shot was made over Cody. He hadn't expected it. He was still thinking offense and wasn't playing aggressive defense. Stung by the lapse, he brought the ball down court, passed off to Gil who passed it back, then in to Ontoveros who was being double-teamed on that side, then took the ball back from Ontoveros and sank a long jumper that brought the crowd once more to its feet.

"C'mon, damn it! Let's get some plays going out there!" Coach was on his feet and following them down the sidelines.

Cody didn't look at him. He didn't want to let anything or anyone intrude on what was happening. He knew it was the most fragile of conditions. If he started thinking about it at all the streak would go away. For now he had to play it out, to take it as far as he could, and he went up the court looking for yet another opportunity to get his hands on the ball and shoot. With the score Coronado 8, Las Cruces 2, Coach called a time-out.

"Boys, we have to start running plays," he told them on the sidelines. "You'll never manage to beat this bunch by depending on the shooting of one man. They've got a guard or two can shoot the same way once they open up. Kid, slack off a little. The rest of you, this here's the state championship. Everybody's got to pitch in and do their part. Brad, you got to move around in there, son, and get yourself open. I don't want to see you camped out in the lane. And when he does, Kid, you and Gil get the ball to him. You're taking way too long. You forwards can help by penetrating the lane. Make 'em come out and guard you to open up that middle. And start putting up some shots, the rest of you. We got to develop two or three hot hands before this evening is over."

Cody listened but he heard none of it. He didn't have to. He had heard it all before and he knew what Coach was saying. He was busy watching the crowd and listening to them, without ever seeing them or hearing them either. Not as individuals but as a collective mass, which by its very lack of individuality bestowed on Cody his. They were in their element, out there somewhere, an entity, the audience; and he was in his, by contrast an individual, made starkly more so by that melded mass of non-individuals looking on. They were the backdrop against which he and his teammates performed; as part of a team, to be sure, but still as individuals, set apart by those individual qualities which had singled them out to be there.

He had always liked spectator sports best; the bigger the crowd the better. He had long ago stepped out of that nameless, faceless mob to assert his individuality, and he never wanted to go back. The more of them there were, the more individual he became. The greater the risk of failure too, but he had long ago accepted that challenge and having accepted it he knew he could never be satisfied with anything less.

He didn't feel any pressure. He was too much in control for that. He felt pressure only when he wasn't confident, or when he couldn't make things happen and tried to force them. But for now he was in control and he felt confident. The feeling was there, and when he put the shots up he knew they would go in.

They took the floor again and he worked to get some offense going. He kept the ball moving until finally Ontoveros broke away along the baseline, getting past his man for a quick lay-up made possible by Brad sagging to the far side of the key and drawing the defense with him. On the next few exchanges Gil scored once from outside, Brad got a turn-around jumper, then Theo hit from the lane. But they merely traded baskets with Las Cruces who managed to get its own offense on track, and each team also missed several shots. Neither side was playing strong defense. Cries of Defense! Defense! could be heard from both benches and the crowd picked up the chant. Las Cruces was not having much success with its man-to-man coverage; on signal from their bench they sank back into a shallow zone to shut off the lane and take away the inside shots.

He knew that the best way to bring them out of their zone was to hit quickly from outside, so he put up a shot from twenty feet that caromed off the rim right into Brad's hands, who went up and banked it in off the glass. It was the first shot Cody had taken following the time-out and he had missed, but he didn't let it bother him. On the next possession he brought the ball down court to the same spot and put up another one, and this one was good all the way.

Three steps before he reached the spot he knew it would go in. He could picture himself in his mind, taking the ball, then two more steps to the spot, planting his foot and turning, then up, and up, hanging there in mid-air, the rim suspended motionless in front of him while the ball rolled off the tips of his extended fingers and traversed the thin narrow space between the basket and his outstretched hand, feeling the shock of the floor in his legs as the net deflected sideways, followed by the soothing, satisfying roar of the crowd engulfing him. Each movement was distinct and indelible, the entire sequence taking place in slow motion. He could not be certain he hadn't just imagined it, as in a dream where every movement is slowed and intensified.

With that basket he was back in the groove. Las Cruces stayed in their zone, and when he couldn't work the ball in to Brad on the next possession he shot once more from the same place and that one too went in. The crowd loved it. They began stomping their feet and chanting in unison, "Two! Two! Two!...," holding up two fingers on each chant. It was a boost for his teammates too. Knowing that someone had a hot hand and could be counted on to carry them past the flat spots took away the pressure and gave them confidence to shoot.

He succeeded in drawing the zone farther out and Brad got a basket underneath on a pass from Theo. Ontoveros drove on the lane from the other side and scored. Then Brad got another turn-around jumper from the low post. When Las Cruces double-teamed Brad, Gil hit Theo along the baseline, who scored from that side. Then, together, they missed five straight attempts, all good shots but none of them falling, before Cody connected on his next two jump-shots to put them right back in it.

At halftime he had twenty-one points. In spite of that the score was tied at thirty-nine. No one else for Coronado was even in double figures. All five of Las Cruces' starters had scored, and three of them had put up double digits.

These two teams were evenly matched. They had split two previous meetings and the total margin of victory in both games combined was only three points. Las Cruces had the more talented and balanced team. Their guards and their forwards were all big men, big enough and good enough to play college ball. Two of them had college scholarships waiting for them and the other two would probably be recruited to play somewhere. But Coronado always had someone who rose to the occasion and made any meeting of these two teams close.

When they came back out at halftime he didn't warm up with the others but sat by himself on the bench staring across the court at nothing in particular. He didn't need to confirm what he already knew, that tonight he had his shot working and when he put the ball up it would go in. The feeling was there as strong as ever and with it he had enough confidence to carry him past any slump. He liked playing the game when it was like this. He liked best the feeling of being in control, the feeling of having done something well—not only as well as he could but as well as anyone could.

This would be his last game. He didn't intend to play in college, or even to go to college right away. He wanted to be away from things for a while. He was too small to play college ball, he thought. You had to be six-six even to play guard in college anymore, and he was barely six-two. Besides, he wasn't the pure shooter that most college coaches were looking for. He might make it on his ball handling; but he had played enough basketball and he had other things he wanted to do. He had proven that he could do this and he knew he couldn't go on playing for the rest of his life so he would quit after this year and try something else for a while.

That was the problem with success, he thought. After you have achieved it you have to keep on achieving it, over and over again. It's not enough to succeed once, you have to succeed the next time too, and the time after that. Success was never lasting. No amount was ever enough. But just one failure could last an entire lifetime. And after success, the only thing left was failure.

He wasn't thinking about that right now, not tonight. Tonight was the way it should be: everything on the line and he was in control. These were the moments he played for, when it all came together and he could make it happen; when the shots fell and he could reach way down deep and pull one out whenever he needed to. This was what success was all about. He guessed he just wasn't constituted to accept failure.

That last morning, he had come and sat beside his father on the bed and told him, without looking him in the eyes and with a distant, small sound in his voice, that if he went through with it he could just forget that he ever had a little boy named Cody. It hadn't been a threat. Cody was just telling him he couldn't accept that kind of failure, that it was a violation of the trust they had always shared. His father knew better than anyone how difficult it was for Cody to say that to him. He had not been surprised by it either. Cody had always been mature and serious beyond his years—too serious at times, his father thought. It was just what he would have expected from him. Cody was not writing him off. He was only letting him know that he felt betrayed. Since that day Cody had had to struggle with the constant contradiction he saw between his father's behavior and what his father had tried to teach him.

They had always been close. His father had been Cody's first coach, and from him he acquired his nickname. When he was small his father had always called him the Kid, and in time it stuck and replaced his real name. When Cody excelled at sports the nickname had seemed like a natural. From his father he acquired his fierce desire to win. He had his father's drive and ambition and attitude. His father had tried to teach him that failure was only bearable if it occurred in spite of everything that could be done to avoid it. It was a philosophy expressed likewise in the corollary that if you tried hard enough there was never any reason to fail. It was a lesson he learned well.

Now so much was changing, so much was uncertain. He didn't like to think about it. Soon the time would come for him to leave too and nothing would ever be the same again. He hadn't accepted that yet, but he realized he couldn't change it either. The only time he saw his father was at the end of each game when he would come by to congratulate Cody on his play. On those occasions his father was ill at ease and never said much. He would say how proud he was of Cody and ask if everything was alright. There were always other people around. The two of them never had a chance to talk before his father would excuse himself and leave. Cody didn't know what to say anymore. Too much had gone unsaid at the time when it should have been said. It would be impossible now to break through the wall of silence built up between them without having it spill over into angry recriminations. That was just another one of the things that had changed. He wondered if his father were here tonight. He knew that he was, but he wondered about it anyway. He never looked at the crowd, not as individual faces, so he never really saw anyone. While he sat thinking about it the buzzer sounded and both teams cleared the floor for the start of the second half.

The coach called them all together in front of the bench and talked to them, but Cody already had his mind in the game. He knew he had to keep scoring, to keep the pressure off the others so they could relax and start hitting their shots. They wouldn't be able to keep Las Cruces from scoring. No one had succeeded in doing that all season. Their only hope was to keep up with them, to keep it close so that at the end they would have an opportunity to win it. All he wanted was that opportunity.

At the tip-off Las Cruces got the ball but he managed to steal it, and as he had at the beginning of the game he put up a long, low jump-shot that ricocheted off the back of the rim and swished through the net. The crowd roared back to life and Cody felt the reassuring warmth of the sound pressing on him from all sides. He scored on each of the next two possessions, but so did Las Cruces.

He set about to get the offense going. He brought the ball down court deliberately and kept it moving, trying to work it in to the open man. He scrapped and fought for every rebound. On defense he directed a full-court press trying to force Las Cruces into turnovers. Through it all he and his teammates played good basketball. Brad moved into double figures, and Theo and Ontoveros balanced out the inside game. When Cody was double-teamed Gil hit from outside or got the ball in to Brad. But Las Cruces matched them basket for basket. No matter how they tried they couldn't seem to open up a lead.

It would at the end be a game of small differences; one explained later by recourse to the statistics of shooting, rebounding, and free-throw percentages; where only a slight edge in one or the other would be cited as the reason behind the win or loss; but he didn't think about that. He was playing not only the last game of his career but his best one too. The feeling was still there, stronger now than ever. He had complete command of his shot, hitting from anywhere on the floor. With it, he kept them in the game. He had played the entire game and he was getting tired yet he still made it look effortless. The crowd knew they were witnessing something special. The chant of "Two! Two! Two!..." broke out again; then "Forty! Forty! Forty!..." as he neared his fortieth point. After that they counted them down... Forty-two!...Forty-four!...as the total kept mounting.

Whereas the first half had been a series of distinct and indelible impressions, the second half gradually smeared into an indistinct and homogeneous blur. He played with no sense of time, no sense of anything but the game itself, of everything that was taking place around him, of being an inseparable part of it. He knew the score not by looking at the numbers on the scoreboard but by the ebb and flow of the game and by the reaction of the crowd. During the last five minutes Coronado hit a flat spot and fell behind by five points, then seven. They cut the lead to five, then, with one minute left, to three; and finally, with two seconds showing on the clock and Las Cruces leading by one point, he was at the free throw line to shoot two.

The first one he put up hit the back of the rim and bounced out. Las Cruces called their last time out.

Las Cruces wanted to give him time to think about this next shot. That didn't bother him; for him it would be like any other shot. He went to the sideline and sat down on the bench, not listening and not hearing what Coach said, not even listening as Coach reminded them there were only two seconds showing on the clock; not listening either when the assistant coach checked with the official timekeeper and confirmed that the time showing on the scoreboard was correct and reported that too. Coach told them that with two seconds left there would be no time for anything but to put the ball back up quickly if the Kid should miss, saying it without looking at Cody who wasn't listening anyway and didn't hear him. Then some final words about rebounding and not mishandling the ball and about tipping it back in quickly if that should be necessary, again said only to the others, not looking at Cody, as if he were not present. Not saying anything to him either as they formed their customary huddle at the buzzer and made ready to go back out on the court because nothing said now could make any difference anyway. At this point it was all up to Cody. No one could take the shot for him or say anything that would help him sink it.

Before the buzzer he sat on the bench not thinking about the shot, knowing already that he would just step up to the line and shoot it like it was any other free throw, like all the ones he had shot before and all the ones in practice, expecting it to go in the same way he expected every shot to go in.

Back on the court he took his place in front of the basket. Without the ball, he raised his arms and went through the motion of shooting, the way he did before each free throw, repeating the follow-through at the end a second time. Then he took the ball and bounced it on the floor exactly four times in what had become his standard routine for shooting free throws, doing it not by counting the number of bounces or by thinking consciously about what he was doing but by some indelible memory imprinted on his senses and in his muscles and triggered now by the bouncing of the ball. The noise of the crowd had swelled once more to a steady roar. He wasn't conscious of hearing it, but he was soothed by the noise; it shut out and isolated him from everything else and helped him concentrate on the shot.

In his mind he imagined himself standing at the line bouncing the ball methodically, deliberately on the floor, then holding it poised above his head and the ball rolling smoothly off the ends of his outstretched fingers as his arms extended effortlessly toward the hoop. He watched as the ball climbed above the basket then descended toward it, hitting the rim and bouncing high above it, suspended at the apex of its arc, motionless, before falling slowly back toward the rim. Suddenly he was standing at the shooting line, his hands still extended in the follow-through position, and the ball was glancing off the right side of the rim. There was a frantic scramble for the rebound and he listened for the sound of the referee's whistle.

The only sound he heard was the buzzer ending the game.

He stood, stunned, not knowing whether he had imagined it or if it had actually happened. The Las Cruces bench emptied and the players were leaping high in the air, hugging each other and dancing wildly about. Then he heard the sounds of the crowd. He heard someone calling his name, then someone yelling, "We're number one," over and over, and someone said, "It's all right, Kid. It's all right." When he looked he could see faces in the crowd, individual faces, the faces of people he knew, and they were talking to him, saying something, or trying to, above the noise of the tumult and the chaos. As he looked he saw more and more faces, heard his name again and again. Many of the faces were looking at him and they were speaking to him. The crowd dispersed into a profusion of individual faces and expressions, all different, some screaming and yelling and jubilant, some silent and inquiring, some frozen in shocked looks of disbelief, but all different; he saw them now not as one mass behind a wall of noise but as individual and separate faces each with its own distinct expression.

Suddenly he spotted his father standing in the crowd and looking at him with that expression he wore when he didn't know what to say or do. He saw his mother too and he knew that the mask of pain and disappointment she wore was for him. He saw Coach trying to make his way off the court, trying to get the team together and into the locker room. Gil and Brad and, one by one, each of his teammates came over to console him, saying something where nothing could be said but saying it anyway before turning away to hide their own pain and disappointment and head for the sidelines. He didn't follow them. He didn't know what to do. He just stood there, hearing every sound, every voice, searching every face in the crowd.

A KNOCK AT THE DOOR

A loud knock at the door startled him causing him to bolt upright in his chair. The hollow veneered door acted like a sounding board, reverberating into the tiny one-room apartment. For the next few moments he was aware of a hard, irregular pounding in his chest and a dull throbbing in his ears as his heartbeat gradually resumed its normal rhythm.

Without moving he took several deep breaths to regain his composure. An uneasy quiet settled over the room. He put aside the book that until a moment ago had held him oblivious to everything else, and leaned forward, quietly lowering the front legs of the chair onto the floor from its position tipped back against the wall.

Around him the dimly lighted apartment was clean but everywhere untidy. Stacks of papers and old receipts littered all but one edge of a dinette table that served also as a desk and work table. Against the adjacent wall the top of a bureau was lined with rows of books several deep. In the opposite corner a large square table held more rows of books stood up on end. Under the table and in the floor beside it were cardboard boxes filled with books and papers that he had never unpacked. Beneath the front windows a long low table was piled with books arranged in narrow columns extending precariously high. The floor from the windows to the center of the room was strewn with other books oriented in random piles on the thin shag carpet, a consequence of nowhere else to put anything. On the wall above a sofa-bed hung a large garish painting done in bright glaring pastels, in grotesque contrast to the dull walls and drab furnishings. Everything about the apartment was old, worn and inexpensive and had a look of incipient squalor.

He sat in the deepening silence, waiting and listening, careful not to make any sound himself. The quiet in the room grew oppressive from a mounting sense of anticipation. Finally, the knock at the door came again, not as loud as before but with greater urgency. He breathed a sigh of relief. This time he was resigned to it.

Crossing to the door and opening it he was surprised to find himself facing the same woman he had encountered three nights ago in the parking lot. Then she had appeared from out of the shadows while he stood fumbling with his keys trying to unlock the car. She had asked for a ride, courteously, but in a manner that left no real option of polite refusal. Though he couldn't see her well in the dim light of the street lamps he knew he had never seen her before. Her request, almost a demand, took him by surprise. He meant to refuse, but he stood mute, and hesitated, and lost his advantage.

He made a feeble attempt to offer an alibi but was met with resolute silence, and under the force of it he capitulated and crossed around the car and unlocked the door for her. Up close he noticed that she was quite attractive, even pretty, in spite of a sullen countenance. Any concern for the plight of a woman that would compel her in desperation to approach a total stranger in a dark parking lot and demand a ride vanished, and he wondered instead if he were the one in danger, a peril he was abetting by his acquiescence. A desperate urge to stop before the matter went any further seized him, but it was too late; he was trapped by his own indecision. The only avenue of escape at this point was blocked by the prospect of an unpleasant confrontation with his silent but insistent passenger, from which he instinctively recoiled.

Why in hell am I doing this? This is how people get in trouble, he told himself. He was not aware that prostitutes worked this area and so far there was no suggestion of anything improper in her behavior. Still, as he drove out of the parking lot he would not have been surprised to see her pull a gun from her purse and declare her real intentions. Instead she indicated that she wanted to go only a few blocks. Except for the simple instructions required to indicate the way, the remainder of the ride was spent in a nervous silence which had become almost comfortable in its familiarity when she motioned for him to stop in front of a small white house and, without further explanation, thanked him and disappeared through the front door. It had all been so unexpected and odd that he had not thought of it again, until he opened the door and found standing before him for the second time a woman that until three days ago he had never seen before.

"May I use your phone?" she asked. She showed no surprise at seeing him. Outside the night air was bitter cold; overhead small puffy clouds illuminated by the combined light of the moon and the city raced across the sky. A few shriveled leaves clinging to the branches of some hawthorne trees rattled in the wind, and light gusts sent clusters of dried leaves rustling along the concrete walk. He searched her expression for any sign that she recognized him but found none. His own face must have conveyed his astonishment at seeing her, he thought; nothing in her manner suggested that she noticed.

"I don't have a phone," he said. Then, because it sounded too much like an excuse and left her at a loss for a response, he added, "but come on in out of the cold."

Once inside she had to step around the piles of books on the floor to allow him room to close the door. Watching her, he was aware of the appalling disarray and shabby appearance of the room. If she noticed she gave no indication. She seemed preoccupied and upset.

"I must call Joseph. Don't you have a phone? Please, it's very important."

"I use the pay phone outside," he said, apologizing that it was inconvenient and uncomfortable in the cold.

"I'm afraid I don't have money for a pay phone. That's why I knocked."

"I have change," he said, producing a handful of dimes and quarters from the end of the dinette table where he kept them stockpiled for those occasions when he needed to use the phone.

He followed her outside without stopping to get his coat and walked with her to the phone booth and looked on as she dialed a number and waited while it rang. Finally, she gave up and replaced the receiver in its cradle. Then she changed her mind and picked it up once more, retrieved the coins from the slot, redeposited them, and dialed again. This time she let it ring longer before admitting there would be no answer. With a shrug of finality she hung up the phone and turned away. He moved over and retrieved the coins from the slot.

"I don't understand why there is never any answer," she said. "I have to find him. Where could he be?" Her question seemed directed to no one in particular.

By now he was getting cold. And she is becoming more upset, he thought to himself. "C'mon," he said, "I have to get my coat before I freeze."

She obeyed, unquestioning. Back inside she sat on the edge of the sofa-bed while he went to the closet and returned with a hooded parka. Then, realizing there was no immediate reason to go back outside, he put the coat across a chair while he waited the next move. She was calm now and seemed contemplative but distracted. She remained sitting on the front edge of the sofa like one unwilling to commit herself.

"Are you sure you have the correct number?" he said. "I have a directory. We can check it." He produced a directory, but it was last year's, and she explained that Joseph roomed with someone who had been here only a short while and the phone was listed in the other name. So he threw on his coat and they hurried back to the phone booth where she looked up the number, which he wrote on a notepad and gave to her along with coins for the phone. He watched as she dialed to insure himself she did it correctly. Again there was no answer and he concluded that she had probably dialed correctly the first time.

When she had hung up the phone she spotted the rows of mail boxes built into the opposite wall of the enclosed walkway that housed the phone booth. Each one had an apartment number displayed on the door and the name of the tenant on a tape label above the box. She searched along the rows of names without finding the one she was looking for.

"There are several other buildings in this complex," he said. "Perhaps he lives in one of the others."

"He is supposed to live here. I thought it should be apartment two twenty-four. I went by there earlier but it was dark." The space above the mailbox for 224 was blank. "Could we look at the other mailboxes?" she said. "Will you show me where they are?" During the next half hour they made the rounds of the other buildings in the complex, examining the names on all the mailboxes to no avail.

Walking back toward his building she repeated, "I was sure he lived in that one, apartment two twenty-four. Let's go by there." There was no one in the apartment. The window was dark and no one answered her repeated knocks at the door.

"I must know if this is the right one," she said. "Will you listen at the door while I go ring the number?" He could hear the phone ringing. She let it ring a long time before it finally ceased and she returned.

"This is the right one all right," he said, "only no one is here." She appeared dejected, and he had been long enough in the cold that his fingers and toes ached and were growing numb. "C'mon, let's go get warm," he said. Overhead the position of Orion in the autumn sky signaled the approach of midnight. The moon was not quite full and was leading Orion in the race westward across the now cloudless sky. A light but steady breeze kept the cold pressed against them as they walked back to the apartment in silence.

He unlocked the door and allowed her to precede him into the room. She again stepped carefully around the piles of books and went straightway to the same seat on the edge of the sofa. She sat, but rose when he asked to take her coat, handed it to him and sat again gazing ahead at nothing in particular. He placed both coats across an empty chair and began shuffling through the stacks of papers on the table in an effort to straighten them but gave it up when he realized he was only drawing attention to a clutter that no amount of rearranging could disguise. He became conscious of how dismal and shabby the apartment looked.

"I'm sorry. I apologize for the mess. I guess I'm not a very good housekeeper. I'm a little out of practice."

"It's all right; I understand. It's so small—and you have so many books." She glanced about her at the piles of books until her gaze came to rest once more on nothing in particular and she sat staring at the floor.

"I'm going to fix hot chocolate. It'll help us get warm again and make you feel better. I can fix coffee or tea if you would prefer. I'm afraid there is nothing here to eat."

"No, hot chocolate would be fine. Please, don't go to any trouble. I really must be going in a moment. I've already taken up enough of your time."

He noticed that for the first time she was looking at him without averting her eyes. He saw again that she was pretty. She looked at him from large oval eyes set wide apart above prominent cheekbones. Her mouth was full and pleasant, permanently on the verge of a smile, her nose fine and narrow and straight, and her jaw square and handsome. Dark hair framed her face and neck. Smooth olive skin concealed her age and the liquid brown eyes were clear and steady. As he looked at her she became self-conscious and dropped her eyes, glancing all about the room before rising and starting over to the bureau against the opposite wall. He could see that she was tall, and though not slender she had long straight legs. He noticed the rounded outlines of her breasts through the thin nylon blouse.

"Are these your children?" She pointed to several small gilt frames standing in front of the books on the bureau. She picked up one that held a photograph of three children and examined it.

"Yes, those three are mine. Taken about a year ago. The oldest is twenty now."

"They are very handsome."

"Thank you, but the credit for that goes to my wife. They have all her best features."

"You are married then? I mean...now?" She seemed surprised.

He hesitated. "Yes, I'm married. He couldn't conceal the slight flush of embarrassment that colored his face under the steady scrutiny of her gaze.

"I'm sorry. I didn't mean to pry. I just couldn't help but wonder. I mean"—she blurted it out—"what's her problem?"

"I suppose I was the problem. Besides, it wasn't her fault. It was no one's fault. It was just something that happened."

"But...you're still married."

When he didn't respond she said, "How long have you lived here?"

He waited before answering. "Quite a few months." He found it difficult to say.

"Then I don't understand. What is her problem?"

He didn't answer. He knew what she was trying to ask. He didn't have an answer.

The chocolate boiled over on the stove, hissing and sending up clouds of steam. He moved the saucepan off the burner and turned down the flame while he reached for a rag, wet it, and wiped the outside of the pan and the top of the stove. He stirred what was left in the pan, placing it back on the burner and reheating it until it once more came to a gentle boil, continued stirring it for a while, then turned off the fire and poured the steaming brown liquid into two large mugs standing on the cabinet beside the stove. She had moved from the bureau over to the stove and stood watching him.

"How old is the youngest?" Her eyes indicated the photographs.

He had to think for a moment. "Let's see, thirteen now, I guess." He carried the filled mugs to the cleared edge of the dinette table, pulled up two empty chairs and motioned for her to be seated. They sat facing the middle of the room their backs to the stove. The piles of books were spread out before them.

"And the girl, is she the oldest?"

"No. She must be seventeen this year. Yes, she will be seventeen." He looked away as if making a mental calculation. "But she looks older, especially in photographs."

"Joseph is eighteen and Maria Teresa is fifteen."

"Then Joseph is your son? The one you were trying to call?"

The inflection in his voice caught her by surprise. She searched his face, trying to gauge his reaction.

"He wanted to live away from home during his final year of school. He found this friend living here who invited Joseph to move in and share expenses. It was close by, and I thought it would be all right. Better than losing him. But I haven't seen him for two weeks; and when I try to call no one ever answers. And twice now no one has been at the apartment."

He tried to reassure her. "I'm sure he must be okay. Probably just keeping late hours. You know how it is when you're that age and have your first real taste of freedom. He'll get tired of it eventually. Is he in school?"

"At St. Ignatius. Maria Teresa sees him at school. And the Fathers would tell me if he weren't going to classes. They know I'm concerned."

"Are you married?"

"Divorced." Her voice invited some response.

"I'm sorry." He studied her face.

"It was a long time ago."

She fell silent and looked far away into the cup at the mottled surface of the chocolate. She cradled the warm cup in both hands, pressing her palms against it along the sides, bringing it close to her and peering down into it so that the warm vapors rose against her face. She sat quietly, breathing the mists from the cup and occasionally sipping the hot liquid. Between sips she remained out of reach, staring into the distance. He watched her for a time, then glanced away whenever he seemed to be staring. After a long silence her attention returned to the piles of books strewn on the floor.

"And you read a lot. What do you read mostly?"

"Anything," he said. "Literature, poetry, novels, history..."

"I like history," she interrupted. "I lived in Europe once, you know. That was a long time ago, too."

"Where in Europe?"

"Italy. Milan and Rome. But we traveled all over. Venice, Florence, Naples. Everywhere."

"Was your husband in the service?"

"His company sent him. At home his parents spoke Spanish while he was growing up. In college he learned French and Italian. So his company sent him over as a sales representative, first in Rome then in Milan."

The distant look vanished from her eyes. In its place he saw something else. He thought he had perhaps discovered what the far away look meant. She spoke eagerly about their life in Italy, and about what she remembered of Rome and Milan and Venice, especially Venice which she had liked best of all and where she had gone often, traveling by herself on the train from Milan to spend the night and to shop and dine and ride in the gondolas. She had been young then and there was only Joseph who could be left with a nurse. Her husband was paid generously for his willingness to live abroad and they were able to live very well, even extravagantly by Italian standards. She had been careful, she assured him, to be generous and fair with the Italians -though it often led to arguments with her husband about money—and they liked her and had not resented her. They liked her, too, in spite of the fact that she never learned to speak Italian well enough to escape notice as a foreigner.

As she spoke her features softened and her face took on a warm glow. The dark brown eyes shown brightly, almost fiercely. She is really very pretty, he thought. This is what she must have been like back then. Twenty years ago I'll bet she was truly something. He could see it in her eyes still, and in her face when she smiled. She must have turned some heads, he thought.

"And, oh, the Italian men. Everywhere I went in crowds I would get pinched and touched—all over." She blushed as she said it. "If you were by yourself they would say things to you, just walking down the street. In the beginning I couldn't understand, but my husband's friends explained it to me." Her husband did not seem to mind, she said, and never objected to all the attention she received. He seemed pleased by it. She too had not minded; she found it flattering and reassuring. It was all innocent enough and it always made her feel good, she confessed, sort of the ultimate compliment of male approval. Later, when she could understand the language better, she had been amused at how ingenious and delicate some of the propositions were. Others made her blush. "There was only once I considered...," but her voice trailed off and she left the statement unfinished.

"We had so much then. We lived in an old stone house surrounded by poplars and ringed with gardens of irises and hyacinths, and there were servants to help with the children and with the meals and the house. I had such pretty things. I went almost every day to the city to shop or to meet my husband for lunch. Or just to find something new to see. Everything was so old and different, and so lovely. There was never enough time to see and do everything..." She paused while pursuing some private thought. The free hand with which she had punctuated the one-sided conversation with animated gestures resumed its position cradling the mug of cooling chocolate. She raised the cup to her lips and held it there, musing, while she drank several swallows of the tepid beverage. When she finished she sat staring without speaking until the silence became uncomfortable.

"How long did you live in Italy?"

"For three years. Until Maria Teresa was born. We both got homesick. The grandparents had never seen the baby, so I made a trip home, which was very expensive. And when I came back with all the news of what everyone had been doing, we both realized for the first time how homesick we were. It was too expensive to go home regularly, or to pay fares for the in-laws to visit us, so we just left."

He saw the far away look return to her eyes. She had placed the almost-empty cup on the cleared edge of the table and was once again peering at the piles of books on the floor without seeing them. He picked up both mugs and without disturbing her slipped back to the sink where he emptied the remaining chocolate into the drain and ran hot water into each cup until the water cleared, then set them aside in the sink to soak. From the cabinet he took two clean cups and a small jar of dark crystals and placed them on the counter top alongside the stove. He turned on the burner under the pan of chocolate and while waiting for it to heat found a clean spoon in the drawer and put a heaping spoonful of the crystals into each cup. He stirred the chocolate until it was steaming, then poured each cup full and continued stirring until all the crystals were dissolved in the chocolate. He placed the pan under the running water in the sink and rinsed it, then turned off the water and left the pan there to soak.

"Here, try this," he said. "No sense letting the rest of the chocolate go to waste." He handed her one of the cups. "Careful—it's hot." She took the cup by the rim in the fingertips of one hand and sat it on the edge of the table. Releasing it, she rotated the cup until the handle faced her and picked it up, with the fingers of one hand on the handle and the other supporting the base.

"Umm, this is good. It's different."

"I put coffee in it. I was going to before, but I wasn't sure you'd like it this way."

"It's very good." She blew the surface of the steaming liquid to cool it and drank several sips with little slurping sounds to keep from burning her mouth. The warm drink had the effect of reviving her.

"What happened afterwards," he said, "after Europe I mean?"

"Afterwards things were never the same. I was determined not to let those three years spoil me—with the servants and all—and I worked very hard. The children were always fed and bathed and ready for bed when he came home in the evenings. I did everything for them so he wouldn't have to do anything. I never let them cry around him or bother him when he was home. We always ate dinner alone, just the two of us, after the children were in bed, and whenever his mother visited I had them bathed and clean. They were such happy children, don't you think?" She waited for him to nod his approval.

"Gradually things changed. He made a lot of money, I suppose. I don't really know. Except that later on he had a lot of money. Then came the divorce and I was never able to understand why. I mean, I did everything for him. The children were always so clean and well behaved, and he had such a comfortable home."

She sat sipping the hot liquid so she wouldn't have to talk anymore.

"What happened to him?" he persisted.

"He married again. He gave the house to me and the children when we divorced. They built a new house. Big and very grand. Joseph and Maria Teresa have told me all about it."

"Do the children like her?"

"Oh yes, she is very young and beautiful, and they adore her. They both used to spend a lot of time there. Maria Teresa still goes nearly every weekend and on holidays, and they take the children on trips with them. I only agreed to allow Joseph to live here because I was afraid he might run away or go to live permanently with his father."

"Tell me," she said, "do you see your children very often?"

"Not often. They live with their mother."

"Why? Don't you want to see them?"

"It isn't that. I don't really think they want to see me. Everyone is still so bitter." He hesitated for a moment. "It hurts too much to see them, the way things are right now. And their mother only makes it..." He stopped short and did not finish what he had started to say. He glanced up to find her looking back at him and he could see that she knew, not exactly what perhaps but at least something of how and why and it made him feel less alone. He felt his eyes burning and he looked away so she would not notice. When he turned back he found her still looking at him and he wanted to reach out and touch her across the gulf separating them, but could not, instead continuing to study her face until finally she looked away and broke the spell.

They sat without speaking until the silence in the room grew at last unbearable. She rose and picked up the cups and carried them to the sink where she ran water in them from the faucet and left them to soak.

"Leave everything. I will wash them later."

"I really must go. I'm very sorry; I didn't mean to trouble you for so long."

He picked up her things from the chair.

"I'll drive you home."

While he helped her on with her coat he assured her it had been no trouble and told her again not to worry about Joseph. He is in school, he told her, and the other is just his new-found freedom and the novelty of it will soon wear off. He donned his parka and turned up the hood.

Outside, the moon shone brightly in the west, casting a yellowish pall over the cloudless sky. Sirius swam straight overhead in the shimmering light and Leo was rising in the east. They walked in silence to the car, where he held the door for her as she climbed in. She didn't ask to go back by 224, he thought to himself. Perhaps she is satisfied, he thought, or maybe she is just tired of problems for now.

"You gave me quite a start the other night in the parking lot. I wasn't sure what to expect."

"Oh, that. I was afraid to walk home alone after dark. You looked honest to me. I didn't know it was your apartment tonight, but I'm glad it was."

As they were leaving the parking lot she said that her mother would be worried, then explained that her mother was widowed and lived with her and the children. The rest of the ride passed in silence, the only sound the clicking of the turn signal and the smooth tearing noise of the tires on the asphalt streets. Only once did he have to let her indicate directions which she did by pointing. After that he recognized the way and found the house again without difficulty.

The porch light was burning—her mother would have left it on, she said—and the yard was bathed by the glow from a street lamp out front. He didn't stop but drove on past the house and along the street, past other similar houses, some set behind low block walls along the street, and a small park with dried brown grass and worn patches of smooth bare earth, turning around in the next intersection and coming back to stop on the opposite side of the street, out of the cone of harsh blue-white light cast by the overhead lamp on the street below. But the real reason, he knew, was otherwise, having nothing to do with the light. He had prolonged it by not stopping but driving on by at the last instant, but couldn't prolong it forever and so turned around and came back, stopping out of the light on the dark side of the road, that way to prolong it further and escape it as long as possible.

She didn't volunteer to leave the car but sat with downcast eyes. The glare from the street light came through the car window onto her face, shadowing the lowered eyelids and tracing her profile with its fine straight nose and full mouth and reflecting from the long ebony hair in glistening streaks of silver. She is really very lovely, he thought to himself. He imagined reaching over and softly touching the thick dark hair, just to touch it, he thought, wondering how she might react if he were to lean over and kiss her, stroking her cheek and neck with his fingertips or running the fingers of both hands like a comb into her hair and pulling her face toward his until their mouths met and were pressed together. In his mind he could taste and breathe and savor her warm delicious scent and feel the soft compliant body pressing against him as he sank deeper into it all along its length, and his senses were swimming with the whirling giddy anticipation of holding her when he became aware of her eyes scanning his face as though she somehow had discerned his thoughts and needed to find in his eyes some clue.

She has prolonged it too, he thought, prolonged it by her silence because she also needed to. Because she is equally uncertain, about what she thinks and wants and what she should do, and about what I was thinking just now and the strange circumstances that have brought us together twice and about the whole mysterious puzzle of everything that never seems to make any sense.

Her eyes came to rest on his and she sat peering past him, as if poised to ask some question, but kept silent instead, perhaps uncertain which one was most likely to yield the answer to all the others. She has as many questions as I do, he thought, maybe more because she has had to live with it longer.

The sound of her voice, as if off somewhere far in the distance, brought him back, and he realized that she had been speaking to him, asking the question she was asking now: "Would you like to go to church with me on Sunday?"

He looked at her for a long time without answering. Why not, he thought, how long must it go on, anything would be better than this; then, hearing the words, as if spoken by someone else, and he, somewhere else, listening to them, but barely able to make out what was being said: "No, I couldn't do that," without offering any reason or excuse, just the plain simple answer which he heard repeated, "I'm sorry, but I couldn't."

A TOUCH OF HUMAN KINDNESS

She rode beside him in the car. Paul was not exactly sure where the meeting was to be held. Or rather he knew the location, but he wasn't sure how to get there. He had a vague, general idea, but he knew that getting there involved a number of connecting roads, poorly marked, and depended on knowing just where to make the right turns. Neither of them had detailed directions. That was the reason she had given for why they should go together. Since neither one of them knew the way, she had asked, couldn't they go in just one car and solve the problem together, only once, rather than separately? That was the reason she gave for calling him. Her voice had sounded almost pleading on the phone.

When she called, Paul thought it odd that she had singled him out. He had met her only once before, recently, and he hadn't known at the time what to make of her. She had come to his office on the pretense of talking to him about her work. Part of it had been about a course she was enrolled in at the college and about a paper she was writing for it. But Paul recalled that much of it had been about her. Little autobiographical revelations that she had subtly interjected, on the unspoken premise that they were relevant and that he should be interested. He hadn't thought anything of that, but he remembered a disturbing intensity and a certain nervous spontaneity about her that had instantly put him on his guard. At times she seemed to seethe inwardly, so volatile and unsettled as to appear in danger any moment of erupting and boiling over, only in the next instant to suddenly subside and become almost passive. At those moments when she flared up she would reach out, place her hand on his arm, and push her face close to his. Her face wore the constant expression of a pained but amazed anticipation. Paul thought the light shining in her eyes betrayed some inner torment. He had no idea why she had picked him to come to for advice. She was Paul's age, he guessed, and maybe she just felt more comfortable confiding in him. Perhaps someone had recommended him, or told her about him, he didn't know.

Now they rode side by side in the darkness, and his mind, only vaguely aware of what she was saying, wandered ahead to the problem of how they would find the way, and to the deeper question of why he had agreed to take her in the first place. Paul didn't even want to go to the meeting. He had given up hoping that anything useful would ever come out of these causes that he allowed himself to get involved in. He had grown tired of people who hated the world, who only wanted to change it to something else without ever understanding what that would mean. In most cases not even something better, Paul thought, just something different from whatever they think is wrong with the way things are. Paul had decided he didn't want to change the world. He didn't know what he would change it to, even if he could. He wanted to live in it, for better or for worse, to experience it the way it was, while there was still time to do so.

He guessed he had agreed they could ride together because it all seemed so improbable when she first mentioned it that he could think of no good reason to say no. He had been caught off guard on the phone. Later, he wished he had refused and offered some excuse, any excuse at all. He thought several times of calling her back and making up some reason after the fact, but he hesitated and put it off until finally it was too late for that. The same uncertainty, the same improbability that made it seem so unlikely at the outset that she would have called him at all kept him from backing out afterwards. There seemed nothing then that he could do about it.

As they rode, she talked about her child. Then about the frustrations of her job, and the problems of being an unmarried mother. The necessity of having to earn a living and the difficulty of balancing her job with trying to take care of everything else that had to be done at the same time. How and why she came to get involved in the various causes she supported. About the difficulty of meeting the right kinds of men, the disappointment of failed relationships. Then about how hard it was to go through life alone, and about herself, her needs as a woman. The topics became progressively personal and private and intimate, all offered very matter-of-factly. As Paul drove, she talked on, circling back whenever he failed to respond but never dwelling on anything long, talking on and on. Not excitedly, but nervously. As if she might erupt and boil over at any moment, he thought.

Gradually, as Paul caught up with his own thoughts, he became aware of what she was saying, and then aware of her and the pent-up and thinly disguised nervousness that threatened at any moment to overflow and spill out into the night. He thought the nervous laugh with which she had begun punctuating her statements was the first sign of an approaching hysteria. She flared up and subsided in unison with the brittle, nervous, choked-off laughs, almost like someone swallowing quiet sobs to cover them up. Then her hand was on his arm, and she leaned closer as the scarcely contained hysteria blazed brightly in her eyes. Her face was close to his. Her voice was reduced to a husky, unbroken whisper.

Suddenly she was telling him—not telling anymore, but confessing to him—that her needs were real. That she was no different from anyone else. That even though she had all these other outlets—her son, her job, the causes for which she worked so hard during every spare moment—she circled back through them repeatedly as he listened—she had other needs too. That her needs were real, the same as everyone else's. She leaned ever closer.

And then, finally, Paul realized what was going to happen. He had not known it before that moment. He knew then that that had been the real improbability, the thing that made it seem odd that she had come to him for advice and even more strange that she singled him out to ask for a ride to the meeting; the thing that had seemed at once so remote and unlikely as to prevent any excuse for why he couldn't take her with him. Once he knew that, he understood everything else too. He saw her now for the first time. For the first time he thought about the things she had been saying to him. He watched as the outline of her breasts moved slowly up and down in the dim light of the oncoming cars. He saw the soft brown hair that framed the shadows on her face, her eyes shining in the reflected light, the look of pained but amazed anticipation. He was no longer apprehensive about the little outbursts, the volatile way she flared up and subsided as she talked, the intimate and personal things that she told him. Any reservations he might have had about her were gone. All concern about finding the way to the meeting vanished. He thought only about what was going to happen. He wondered how she would respond. He returned her touch and lightly put his hand on her breast. He brushed his fingers softly across her cheek.

She was not talking anymore. When he glanced over at her she had leaned her head back against the seat and was staring straight ahead. She closed her eyes and seemed to shudder slightly, as if sobbing quietly inside. Then she was still.

THE PARTY

They decided to go to the party anyway, in spite of the fact they both knew what kind of party it was going to be. In spite of that, and because of it too. They had decided to go, and agreed to go, which meant, among other things, that they agreed to accept whatever happened as a consequence.

That was the nature of the understanding between them about everything. Before they married they drew up a prenuptial agreement—one that asserted and affirmed the only real precondition, and the one fundamental basis, on which the marriage was made. "The underlying principle of our relationship is that we pledge ourselves each to honor and respect the independence and individuality of the other, even in the union of marriage...", it began. He had written it; she had asked him to. They had both freely endorsed it. Marriage based on the freedom to maintain their independence and keep their individuality intact was the only kind of marriage either of them could imagine, and the only kind either of them would have accepted.

Janet's parties were well known. She had a steady clientele of couples. That was one of the rules. The invitations were to couples, though not necessarily married, and singles were sometimes invited but were required to bring someone of their choosing, or—and Janet was not above this—someone whom she specifically designated, someone who regularly attended and participated in the goings-on.

It was the goings-on that made Janet's parties so well known. She and her husband had agreed at the start of their marriage to tolerate each other's extramarital affairs. Without such an accommodation there could have been no marriage. Jim was a successful divorce attorney, handsome, six figures, with a penchant for sleeping with his clients as part of the total package. Janet had been one of his conquests when she came to him for a divorce brought on by her own promiscuity. She had tried to get her former husband to make the same arrangement she and Jim entered into—she knew he had affairs with other women, including some of her best friends—but he in turn couldn't handle what Janet was doing even though that didn't go so far as to keep him from doing it. She actually had Jim propose just such a formal arrangement to her then husband, as the basis for some sort of reconciliation. Subsequently it became the cornerstone of her marriage to Jim.

Experimenting—that's what they both considered it since otherwise they were totally committed to one another—with other sexual partners came to be such a part of their marriage that they decided to make it a part of their social life together too. When they entertained, which they did frequently, it was understood that there would be opportunities during the evening for couples to pair off as often and in whatever way they wished.

Their house had been chosen with that in mind. In addition to the downstairs bedrooms, the entire upstairs had been remodeled after they bought it, into bedroom and bath suites, each with its own entrance opening onto one of several foyers reached by separate sets of stairs. By being at all discrete and observant and the least bit careful in timing, one could come and go without being the object of unwanted attention.

Not that one would be anyway. That was another of the rules. Anyone who became overly curious about the comings and goings of the guests, especially anyone whose interest caused outward comment or complaint from one of the other guests, was not invited back. Janet was very attentive and solicitous in the matter of her guests' behavior. Couples who came together were not to remain together beyond the initial introductions and preliminary small talk, but were expected to separate and mingle so that they were accessible to the other guests. Beyond that the only rule was that anyone was free to refuse any advances made—no strings attached. There was never to be any coercion beyond the usual discrete innuendos and expressions of interest.

Those guests who did not follow the rules or who did not take part were at some point not invited back. Janet knew what went on—she made it her business to know—though she adhered to a strict code of not gossiping and never divulging a confidence, other than using something she had learned to her advantage in arranging subsequent gatherings.

Janet and Jim had ceased to derive their primary stimulation from the sexual encounters their parties brought them. Instead they had come to cherish the successful conduct of these gatherings as their chief gratification. Both of them had become much more circumspect in their own sexual conduct, in the course of managing these affairs and working to insure the enjoyment of their guests, than they would have been as mere participants. In time, they had found the vicarious sexual pleasures they derived more stimulating and more fulfilling than the actual thing.

Janet, especially, worked constantly to infuse new life into these occasions. That meant finding new couples, or at least new partners. Inviting singles and allowing them to choose someone to bring carried an additional risk, so she usually tried to invite couples or to find both members of any singles she invited. In this enterprise she made use of anything and everything she had learned from, or about, her guests and their friends. Before she ever approached anyone with an invitation she made certain that they already knew the nature of the arrangements and were likely to be flattered, or at least not offended, by being invited, even if at first they didn't feel comfortable accepting. She was gracious and understanding if her invitation was declined on the first offer and found some way of extending it again, and even again, without seeming presumptuous or overly forward. At some point, when she felt the prospects were sufficiently attractive, she extended an open invitation and left it standing.

That had happened in their case. They knew about Janet's parties long before they were ever invited to attend. Cynthia worked in the attorney general's office. She had met Janet because of Jim and had instantly liked her. That initial felicity turned into a secret admiration when she learned later that Janet was the one who threw the parties they had heard about. Not that either of them imagined themselves involved with that group. Yet there was enough of a streak of rebellion and non-conformity in both of them to harbor a secret, almost grudging, envy of those who did attend.

When they were first invited Paul declined for both of them without even discussing it beforehand with Cynthia. If the object of the revolt had been anything besides sex he could have imagined Cynthia perhaps interested. Sex—as a thing apart from their marriage—did not seem to hold any particular fascination for her. They had a perfectly normal and, as far as he was concerned, a healthy and open, if somewhat inhibited, sexual relationship. Cynthia didn't seem wild about sex but still required it. He thought she used sex mostly to gauge his continued interest in her. If the frequency of their lovemaking fell off too much she became concerned and solicitous, although she seemed too easily satisfied for it to have been much of a real craving. She had not been a virgin when they married and had already had several long-standing sexual relationships, mostly with men for whom she later seemed to have little respect. Perhaps that was the problem, he sometimes thought. But it wasn't a problem really so he never dwelt on it beyond wondering if she truly enjoyed sex or merely tolerated it.

That was the real problem. The inhibition was not so much in what they did together but in their inability to talk about it with each other. She had always seemed willing to do whatever he initiated, but she seldom took the initiative herself and never suggested what she wanted from him. Perhaps after a while everything that can be said about it has been said and it's better to just go ahead and do it, Paul thought. Still, her reticence to talk about it nagged at him and left him suspicious and dissatisfied.

He wondered if something like this happened to all couples. After a while there is nothing more to say or do that has not already been said and done. After all, how many different ways of making love are there and how many different ways of talking about it; before you both just get bored with the same old thing all the time and start looking for someone with whom you haven't done the same things over and over and said the same things about it again and again. Someone with whom there is still some spontaneity and freshness and the anticipation of something new and unexpected and exciting. Some new adventure, something unknown to explore.

He knew better than to try to change her. This is how she is, he told himself; that's part of the mystery of any relationship. It was that mystery he admired most about her; the depths and the strengths and the unanticipated twists and turns of her makeup. He was still learning about her complexity and mystery, and he was always a bit off-guard as a result. He never assumed that he understood her or knew the real truth of anything about her, and he liked that. It meant that almost anything was possible, that all the options were still open, and she remained alluring and attractive to him on that account.

Not long after the first invitation, Cynthia told him one morning that they had been invited again. Janet had called and mentioned she was sending them an invitation. No need to reply immediately, think about it, she told Cynthia; but they sent their regrets. They didn't seriously consider it, or even discuss it, except to express a sort of nervous amusement. Both of them professed to be uninterested, although Paul found himself wondering what it might be like. Cynthia sensed his curiosity and kidded that maybe he would like to go and participate. Go perhaps, but not participate, he had said, and they had not discussed it any further.

Other invitations followed, always with a note that said no reply was necessary, come if you can. But always they declined, at first by phone then after a time by sending thank you notes. Privately Paul felt uneasy that they did nothing to discourage any further invitations even while they assured themselves they were not interested. Cynthia, he believed, was pleased and flattered by the attention, and neither of them seemed to want to completely let go of the possibility that they might actually do this. Finally Janet, whom Paul had never met but felt he knew, telephoned and told him that they had a standing invitation and that she would keep sending notices of future parties. "Please try to come," she urged him. "We would love to have you, and remember, there's no obligation," she assured him, then left it at that.

And then at some point they had simply decided to go, and agreed to go, and neither of them really knew why beyond the fact that they had decided they would go without ever talking about it and afterwards it became one of those things they couldn't—or didn't—talk about, and the decision stood. The agreement that, once there, they would be free to do whatever they wished was understood. Without it, no decision to go would have been possible, the same way they did everything. About that no discussion was necessary.

Cynthia even teased Paul he was free to join in, though he imagined she said it more in self-defense than anything else. Paul knew that he wouldn't. That wasn't why he was going. But the thought that he could, that he was free to, that was part of it; that made it more interesting. Without that he might have no interest in going at all. That remote possibility, however slight, was what touched his imagination and intrigued him. He knew that Cynthia wouldn't participate either, but that same remote possibility left the unlikelihood no less intriguing. Still, for Paul, it was the realization that neither of them would actually get involved that made the whole thing thinkable.

And they had arrived and Jim had taken him off to get a drink, but not before Paul kissed Cynthia lightly on the cheek while she had whispered in his ear, "I think we are supposed to separate and mingle among the guests," and Janet had whisked her away to meet some of the other women. There were six other couples there, not counting the hosts, and as Jim showed him around the house—all quite unobtrusively and nonchalantly, never offering any rationale or explanations, as though Paul were as experienced in the goings-on as all the regular guests—Paul noted that there were more bedrooms than couples. He didn't know any of the other guests, which was exactly the way he preferred it, though he imagined that one or two looked familiar. At least none of them had been in any of the classes he taught or were people he had to encounter on a regular basis.

Now that he was here Paul felt ill at ease and out of place. Perhaps it was just in stark contrast to the warmth and size of the house, or perhaps he only imagined it, but it seemed to him a somewhat subdued group, in marked contrast, he thought, to the affability of the hosts who were circulating about attentively and talking to everyone.

Paul and Cynthia had been the last to arrive—though they had timed their arrival to precisely the time Janet had specified—and the men were still mostly off by themselves on one side of the room while the women had collected on the other side or were out in the kitchen helping Janet. Paul discovered that most of these couples did not know one another, though most appeared to have been here before and all of them seemed familiar with Janet and Jim. After two drinks he gradually warmed up to them. As far as he could see there was no common thread to what these people did for a living or where they worked or why they would have known, or been known by, Janet or Jim. He listened a good deal more than he talked, which was his manner, and because he wanted to stay in charge of what he chose to reveal about himself.

Paul was dressed as he always did, properly but casually in coat and tie, which made him fit right in. One of the men had worn a tuxedo, which in his case did not strike Paul as out of place since it served to cover up what was otherwise a stout and muscular but rather coarse appearance. The man had come with a tall, stunning dark-haired woman who was dressed in a revealing but tasteful and flattering black evening dress. Her eyes, Paul thought, were especially riveting. They had that peculiar quality of transfixing whomever they looked at, and the capacity to leave the object of their gaze ill at ease. At one point he noticed Cynthia talking to her. The man in the tuxedo was quiet but without any suggestion of shyness. He seemed engaged and intent but proper and well mannered. Later, when the man went over briefly to talk to the dark-haired woman, Paul noted that, together, there was an intensity about them that he found unmistakable and disturbing. Still, Paul thought she was easily the most attractive woman there.

For the first hour or so nothing much happened. One or two of the men wandered off but came back shortly with more drinks and joined back in the conversation. Neither Jim nor Janet made much attempt to break it up. The women by now had for the most part drifted off in small groups, some with Janet and some to wander in and out and about the other parts of the house. Finally at some point several of them helped Janet bring out a buffet after which there was a new round of drinking and Paul noticed several of the men mixing with the women. Gradually, as he watched, the guests began to mingle and then disperse into smaller mixed groups and pairs. He saw Cynthia talking with the dark-haired woman.

Then, almost as if on cue, Jim took Paul downstairs to the game room to see his collection of guns. Jim had a Purdy, an early vintage L.C. Smith, a model 21 Winchester—all guns Paul had shot at one time or another, but not often enough that they had lost their fascination—plus an assortment of other pieces which Paul admired, handled, and then replaced while he and Jim swapped stories. Here, Paul could hold his own. Jim had already determined that Paul was not likely to join in, and he was too solicitous a host, having concluded that, to leave Paul to his own devices for the entire evening.

Later, when they came upstairs, the lights were dimmed, there was loud music playing, and a few couples were dancing. Several of the dancers were drunk on their feet. One couple, her hands on his hips and his on her breasts, were rubbing against each other lewdly. Others sat and talked, and one or two wandered off by themselves. A striking but very inebriated blond in a low-cut dress came over to where Paul sat and, leaning over him, pushed her breasts against his face as she reached down to kiss him on top of the head. She then turned and walked away, looking back once as she left the room and disappeared into a hallway.

Paul had to relieve himself and went off in search of a bathroom. The hall was darkened, and as he started down the corridor toward where he remembered seeing a bathroom earlier, he became aware of someone in the dark in front of him. Startled, he stopped. Paul recognized the man in the tuxedo and the dark-haired woman with him. Between them, holding each by the hand and accompanying them down the hall toward the open bedroom at the end, walked

Cynthia; like a little child, Paul thought, accompanying adults, obediently and without suspicion.

He stood stunned and watched in silence, unable to speak or move. Cynthia was going freely, not following but accompanying. At the end of the hall the man in the tuxedo paused, motioning with a sweeping gesture of his left hand for the two women to enter the darkened room. He then followed behind them without looking back and slowly, quietly shut the door. Paul stood bewildered and heard the tongue of the bolt click into the face plate, then the metallic snap of the latch. He remained where he was in the darkened hallway, listening, unable to think or move. No light appeared beneath the door, and no sound came from the room. Paul felt drained and empty. There was a tightness in his chest and a hollow, sinking feeling in the pit of his stomach. He became aware of his heart pounding. He could hear his own breathing, shallow and rapid. He felt cut-off, isolated, excluded from everything around him.

For a moment he tried imagining that he was the one accompanying Cynthia down the hall, but when he did he couldn't picture the other woman. When he tried to, he saw the woman leading Cynthia into the darkened bedroom and the man, waiting, closing the door behind them. He heard again the metallic click of the latch, sharp and distinct in the silence of the hall. Beyond that there was nothing. He tried to force himself to imagine something beyond the closing of the door, beyond the darkness of the room and the blank, empty silence, but he could not. No images came, only the hollow feeling in the pit of his stomach and the tightness in his chest. It was that void, that black unknown where no images formed and where his experience could not take him, that made the tightness in his chest feel as if it would cut off his breath and cause him to suffocate.

Quietly, as if to escape all notice himself, Paul went along the dark hall to the bathroom. He closed the door and splashed cold water from the faucet over his face and neck. The cold water against his face revived him and let him breath freely again. Paul looked long at the drawn, ashen expression in the lighted mirror as he wiped his face with a towel. He was aware that something was terribly wrong but he could form no clear idea of what it was. There was the same void in his thoughts that had been there when he tried to get beyond the closed bedroom door.

Paul turned off the bathroom light and stood in the dark, listening. He was now swallowed up in the void, and it seemed to offer him the only escape possible, that of isolation from all sound and all images. But the empty, hollow feeling crept slowly back and would not let him escape. Paul opened the bathroom door, listening to make sure no one was in the hall. Then he quietly went to the closed bedroom and stood for a moment at the door and listened. He heard nothing. He felt defensive and guilty about standing there trying to listen, to eavesdrop on what was going on behind the closed door. He knew that was against the rules, a violation of what he had agreed to when he decided to come. Paul made his way back down the hall.

He felt suddenly self-conscious. He went into the kitchen and poured himself a scotch, drank part of it, then refilled the glass. He wanted to just stand there all alone and drink his scotch, but he couldn't. Paul couldn't imagine anything he could do that didn't draw unwanted attention to himself. He dreaded the thought of going back into the other room where he would be seen, where he might have to talk to someone. He didn't know if he would do, or say, something foolish.

He was still alone in the kitchen when Janet found him. "I can't tell you how pleased we are that you came and brought your lovely wife." With one hand she gently rubbed the small of his back, then she leaned forward and lightly brushed her lips against his. "Now that you two have been here I do hope you'll come again," she said. Her perfume and the whiskey and the empty feeling in his stomach caused a wave of nausea to sweep over him. Janet reached down and took his hand and gently squeezed it before walking away as quickly as she had come.

Somehow, he got back into the other room unnoticed and sat by himself, watching the couples who were still dancing. Everyone else was gone from the room now. Twice he saw couples disappear up the stairs, once together, and once separately a few minutes apart even though they had been dancing together just moments before. He was thankful now for the loud music which helped obscure and draw attention away from him. Two women tried to engage him in conversation, and one of them, a woman who reminded Paul of Cynthia, he talked to until a man came over and invited her to dance. When he looked for her again the two of them were no longer there.

After a while he saw the man in the tuxedo dancing with the other woman Paul had been talking to, and shortly they too were gone from the room. He talked to some of the other guests but he couldn't remember which ones, and he went back once to the kitchen for another drink but he couldn't remember that very well either. Soon afterwards Paul heard Cynthia's voice, then saw her in the kitchen with Janet. She was smiling and the two of them were talking as if they were old friends. In a few minutes Cynthia came over. "Janet said you were not looking well," Cynthia told him. "All you all right, Paul?"

Paul rode home in silence. Cynthia related some of what she had learned about the guests and Paul tried to feign interest, but he heard very little of it. As she talked he found that he could not even remember most of the guests, though he tried to. The details of the evening were slipping away from him, leaving him with a blank, like the void that had engulfed him as he stood in the dark silence outside the closed bedroom door and tried to get past it in his mind. In its place a comforting emptiness was taking shape.

For now, he knew that he shouldn't try to get past it. It is all part of the mystery that made her so alluring and intriguing to him, Paul thought. This was no different from any of the other things in her past about which he knew nothing and about which he preferred instead to imagine whatever made her more appealing and desirable. He realized that he had not really wanted to penetrate that void and know what he could not change anyway, and wouldn't even if he could because he would not know what to change it to, what to put instead in its place. They had decided and agreed, the way they did about everything. He couldn't start changing that now, not in this case, not without changing everything else as well. She had come back to him even more mysterious and more intriguing, and the hollow feeling in the pit of his stomach and the tightness in his chest had only been his fear about whether he would be able to cope with the mystery, with what he couldn't ever know or begin to understand.

Then at some point he was aware that Cynthia was no longer talking and hadn't been for some time. "Paul," she said finally, "are you sure you're all right?" He looked at her, searching her face, but there was nothing there.

HOUSE OF MIRRORS

Every room in the house had mirrors on the walls. Not modest individual mirrors tastefully framed and hung like paintings or pieces of decorative art, but whole walls wainscoted and covered completely from floor to ceiling, from baseboard to cornice and from corner to corner, with unbroken, unseamed expanses of silvered glass swimming with lambent liquid reflections even in the faintest light. Not for purposes of utility as in bathrooms or above vanities, nor for decorative effect in dining room or hallways, nor even for the appearance of luxury and elegance in living room or bedroom; but in every single room of the house, mirrors on the walls. And not on every wall. But always on that wall to which attention was naturally drawn first upon entering the room or space. As if mirrored images composed both the form and substance of every object and everyone and every action taking place there. And also on the wall immediately opposite, or adjacent, so that the images visible in each were repeated endlessly in the other, ad infinitum, giving to the room an aspect of unbounded space and to every movement in it a myriad of mirrored movements receding rectilinearly into the limitless distance, multiplying every microcosmic feature into an ever-expanding macrocosm.

In some rooms the mirrors consisted of plain silvered glass without special adornment or decoration, beyond the undistorted images plainly visible in its depths. On other walls were mirrors adorned with spidery webs or strands of gold and silver filigree woven and tangled about the images embedded in the glass. Some were of antique glass, wavy and uneven in thickness and optical quality, chosen for the slight but intended distortion of images, as if mirroring a reality that had gone somehow slightly out of kilter. Still others were, in places, concave or convex, making fat thin or thin fat, and tall short or short tall, imparting to the depiction of reality a bizarre and comic twist that rendered even the commonplace and mundane more interesting and intriguing. Mirrors lining the opposite walls of narrow hallways rendered each a kaleidoscope of color and motion at the smallest movement. There where walls were not flat, but swayed and bowed or met the floor or other walls unevenly, the world mirrored leaned and bulged or contracted and expanded in ways that lent an appealing aura of imperfection and credibility to the reality portrayed by the images.

All of this could of course be somewhat disorienting to someone experiencing it for the first time. Guests at first were constantly running into things while trying to negotiate spaces whose depths were mere illusion. Or while trying to traverse doorways and passages that existed, only elsewhere than where they initially appeared. Some would occasionally stumble or trip and would have to glance often at their feet to steady themselves. Some found the repeated images of their surroundings dizzying and unsettling and could not locate themselves or focus on their own figure among the endless array of forms. For others it was necessary to stand or sit quietly at first, avoiding any sudden movement while they positioned and oriented themselves in their newly expanded world.

For most however it was ultimately liberating, even enriching. One no longer felt confined or constrained within a space bounded by walls, but seemed positioned instead at the center of an expanse opening ever outward without limit. Awareness of walls vanished, and the receding interior merged with the openness and vastness of the surrounding desert. One did not go into the house so much as to a location in the desert around it. One quickly learned that shadows as well as objects have both color and shape, and the leanings and waverings and distortions of the mirrored reality more accurately mimicked those of the local surroundings. Irony became a way of thinking and a natural way of seeing. Contrast, conflict, even contradiction, no longer startled or disconcerted, but amused and entertained and enticed one to see the unanticipated surprise in place of the expected humdrum. Awareness became heightened and sensitized as every movement no matter at first how small or innocuous promised to surprise and delight and to reveal those secrets of perception that illuminate and enhance reality. Illusion itself became not contrary to reality but its raison d'etre and guiding principle. One could no longer passively regard one's surroundings. To be able to see at all, interaction was tantamount.

It had not always been so. When they bought the house it was quite ordinary, even old-fashioned. The space inside was all sectioned off into adjacent little boxes cobbled together by walls and narrow doorways and passages. One felt always comfortably caged, but caged nevertheless, shielded and alienated from all but an artificial rendition of reality. Their first thought of remedy had been to tear down walls and open up the interior of the house. But the most likely candidates were all load bearing and could not be removed without major restructuring. Those that could be taken out did not relieve the situation.

A physicist by training and profession, he thought of mirrors. His idea was to provide at least an illusion of openness. Little did he anticipate the success of the scheme or the scope and complexity of the effects achieved.

He studied the interior geometry of the house and considered the laws of geometric optics governing the reflection of light and the appearance and position of images in mirrors, both opposing and angled, flat and curved. Then he began experimenting. He chose the walls he would have removed if free to do so and covered them instead with mirrors, replacing them with images seen in opposite or adjacent walls similarly clad in silvered glass. Almost miraculously the mirrored walls vanished, replaced by a cascading sequence of identical scenes receding and ever diminishing into the indefinite distance. The image of any object placed alongside the mirrors was multiplied a thousand-fold until it became not a solitary object in the room itself but a characteristic feature of all space between it and the now vanished wall as far as the eye could follow. The room no longer held the objects it contained. Instead it was filled by a boundless and endlessly created expanse permeated by countless reproductions of objects distributed uniformly as far as one bothered to survey.

They soon learned a few simple rules of decorating that enabled them to create the new reality they wished to achieve. At first it was they who by the choice and placement of objects in the rooms shaped the appearance of reality around them. But at some point the illusion of reality they were creating for themselves began to shape, or rather reshape, them as well.

He liked to sit in the dwindling light of the desert dusk shining through an uncovered window and contemplate the few simple rules of physics that applied over and over in unending iterations to the images of simple objects could create such bewildering complexity and startling variety. He would find an appearance that he couldn't immediately fathom, and puzzle it out until either it finally became too complex for him to trace any further in his mind alone, or he became eventually persuaded that it did indeed agree with his understanding of the rules governing how light behaved.

He found himself drawn not to what he was able to understand and make sense of, but to what seemed almost to defy his comprehension. At first as a puzzle he was bent on solving, convinced as he was of its simplicity if only he could determine how to look at it correctly. It was an exercise in mental and intellectual agility, a game he played against himself in the beginning. But he soon tired of it, finding that he much preferred to enjoy and contemplate the complexity than any game of ratiocination that tried to dismiss it and substitute in its place a few simple principles. The principles ultimately explained nothing anyway. They merely replaced one set of puzzles by another set equally puzzling. He knew that all he could hope for was to describe the world. He gave up long ago on the possibility of ever going beyond that to any kind of deeper understanding.

He wasn't sure he would want that even if it were possible. The world was strangely diminished by facts. Facts were not, he knew, the answers to real questions. They were not the answer to any question at all. If it could be answered it wasn't truly a question. Real questions had no answers – that is what made them questions. Facts were just facts, that which can be known about the world, even if only provisionally. And that, he knew, was pitifully little compared to the mystery remaining. He had since moved beyond facts, to acknowledge – and embrace – the mystery.

As he sat each evening in the languishing light of dusk rendered almost liquid by the crystal reflections from the mirrors on the walls, facts faded from his view, replaced by fantasy. He became less aware of the world as macrocosm and more drawn to the microcosm around him. He felt the magic and wonder of space and time extended and multiplied in every direction, until his immediate world became the whole world filled with the fantasy of its every detail and imperfection. The ever-startling surprise of the unanticipated distortions and imperfections in the mirrored images surrounded and immersed him in a reverie of child-like fantasy. His thoughts turned from facts to fiction, from a literal, rigid reality to open contemplation of spontaneous possibilities. Maxwell's equations and quantum electrodynamics gave way to Alice in Wonderland and Through the Looking Glass. Fictional characters loomed suddenly large in his thoughts and became the standard of comparison. Reason retreated.

Conformity lost all appeal; in its place numerous little heresies sprang up.

There was no escaping the images, no escaping the reality shaped by the mirrors on the walls. Life in Casa de Espejos became transformed by the reality experienced there. The combination of fantasy and elegance, of openness and freedom, of the richness of detail and the crystalline brilliance and luxuriance of light and color produced a palpable sensuality and voluptuousness that could be felt as well as seen in every room of the house. Only in the total darkness of some remote corner or recess could one think to escape it, and not even then escape but only diminish it. One was never alone. Every presence, every movement was accompanied by countless images. Nothing no matter how furtive was hidden from view. Every action was displayed in multiple versions from many angles and vantages. Secrecy and hiding were futile. Deception became reality and reality deception.

Though retreat was instinctual at first, it soon gave way to candor and freedom and complete loss of inhibition. What could not be covered up and disguised was better exposed and brought out into the open to be confronted and examined. The time they spent alone together became richer and fuller as it became less inhibited and more intimate, as it more closely came to resemble the fantasy mirrored in their surroundings. When they were together, each could see not only the other, but in the mirrors also themselves, not as they were accustomed to seeing themselves, alone, but in the presence of the other, and as they each knew that the other was accustomed to seeing them in return.

Whatever latent narcissism each felt in the presence of their own image was transferred to the other also and became a mutual shared narcissism. They liked seeing themselves together. They liked to touch and they liked to watch themselves touching and being touched in kind. They derived a sensual erotic pleasure from being surrounded and immersed in the rich visual imagery of their intimacy as well. Since nothing could remain hidden all attempts were abandoned and everything was fully exposed and indulged for their mutual pleasure and satisfaction. Their shared narcissism mirrored the subtle complexity and fantasy of their surroundings.

Their life took on a new passion and intensity and, ironically, a new contentment. All difference, all dispute was quickly exposed and openly displayed and just as quickly set aside. Each became the object of the other's passion and desire for themselves, against which all other concerns became secondary. They spent more and more time together and more time alone in the house. Evenings, mornings, even whole days would often pass without them emerging except for the briefest and most perfunctory of excursions. Those who had experienced for themselves the fantasy and magic of the rooms adorned with mirrors came to realize its inescapable sensuality, even its eroticism. But only a few intimate acquaintances ever fully comprehended the true meaning of the little red satin pillows, each embroidered in the very center with a gold braid heart, that adorned the floor and furnishings of the most visually stimulating and enticing places in every room of Casa de Espejos

THE NOSE

Let me tell you—something is wrong. Something is definitely wrong. On the other hand maybe I am only mistaken and everything is really all right. If I seem confused you must excuse me—it may simply be the result of whatever is wrong. At this point I'm not sure anymore.

They certainly haven't been able to find out. Or if they have, they haven't told me. I think they are probably as confused and mystified by it all as I am. They would deny it of course and try to pretend that they understand and have everything under control. But they don't fool me. Not for a minute. They may actually believe they do understand, but if so it is only because they have succeeded in fooling even themselves.

I first detected that something was wrong—with my nose. I smelled trouble. Perhaps that is why no one believed me. They didn't realize that you can still sometimes smell trouble. Who, after all, believes anymore in the senses? It would be most unreasonable to trust such crude and outmoded evidence. It would be tantamount to admitting that one doesn't understand.

Nevertheless I smelled something amiss. All at once everything had a pungent aromatic odor about it, sharp and slightly metallic, musty even. Mediciney you might call it—like something purchased at the pharmacy or concocted in a chemistry lab. I smelled it everywhere, always the same. No one else smelled anything. "Don't you smell that," I asked them? They just shook their heads and stared at me suspiciously. The suspicion soon gave way to looks of pity, or even worse—disgust—as though they were all aware of something that I alone didn't realize and couldn't comprehend. When I persisted they looked at me sadly and turned away.

After a while I began to suspect that the problem was with

my nose. That somehow it was stuck on a false signal which it was generating and sending to the brain, a signal that the brain in turn was interpreting as the strange chemical odor that I smelled everywhere. That would have been a reasonable explanation—one based on a hypothesis that at least took into effect how the body works—and it would have accounted for why I was the only one affected. Even if it were wrong such an explanation made sense out of things and restored to the world its assumed order and harmony. I suppose that's why I found it so appealing. Even they were inclined to agree with me when I first suggested it. They seemed to prefer that explanation to all the other possibilities that came to mind.

There were other reasons to suspect the nose. It hadn't been the same ever since the surgery. A knife-happy, ear-nose-and-throat man who never saw a nasal septum that he didn't declare deviated had talked me into it. He and the buxom nurse who assisted him in his legalized larceny told dirty jokes the whole time in the operating room, which set me to wondering about the propriety of it all. But the marvelous little pill they gave me to take the edge off my day, before administering the local anesthetic, took away all my inhibitions and put me in the mood to willingly participate in my own execution, if asked. The nurse had nice round boobs which she kept dangling just in front of me and shoving in my face whenever she leaned forward. It seemed the more she did it the more frequent and pronounced and prolonged it became. I wanted to reach up and squeeze one, like a big piece of ripe fruit, but they must have had my hands tied down or else I couldn't get my thoughts focused long enough to keep my mind on it.

The surgeon was from a locally prominent family whose name was Italian—the same as a famous manufacturer of men's fine dress shoes—which you would instantly recognize if I were to mention it. Afterwards I could not look at a pair of wingtips without being reminded of licensed greed, and suffering a general feeling of revulsion. As a result I took to wearing only running shoes for all occasions, and I gave up suits and ties altogether. My taste in shoes eventually led me to discover the music of Willie Nelson, which in turn changed my life forever. I became drawn to the quirky lyrics and haunting melodies of songs that actually had something to say. I began to think about things that until then had gone completely unnoticed and unexpressed in my life. I suppose you could say I became more aware, more thoughtful. And, yes—more suspicious. After the surgery I could breathe freely, to be sure, and my sinuses drained better than before; but now I smelled trouble everywhere. "Don't you smell that," I kept asking them? They just looked at my running shoes and open-neck shirt with no tie, and no coat, and shook their heads in bewildered amazement.

Perhaps it was the music. Or maybe it was because the blood flowed more freely to my head now, unimpeded any longer by those formal strictures with which we bind ourselves into merely decorative but no-less-obedient conformity. Or maybe it was simply that my feet didn't hurt anymore. At any rate, whatever the reason, one day it dawned on me. I suppose it would be more appropriate to say, in the manner of the active voice that is so fashionable these days, that suddenly I smelled it. With my nose I sniffed out the truth.

I was listening to music by Lyle Lovett, John Prine, Jerry Jeff Walker, and David Allen Coe, and to some blues singer who doesn't count and will remain nameless since I couldn't understand a thing he was saying anyway. The blues singer kept repeating everything he said, which in his case was neither pleasing nor poetic but merely resulted in twice as much pointless screaming. When all at once my nose caught a whiff of it. Perhaps it wasn't my nose that was malfunctioning. Not at all. And perhaps the surgery wasn't to blame either. Maybe what I smelled was just the truth. Maybe the surgery had somehow fixed my nose to where it finally worked the way it should.

Breathe deeply, the surgeon had commanded, after he removed the gauze packing my nose. At that first inhalation I felt as though my lungs would explode. The air gushed in as my chest shot forward. I could feel my sternum tugging at my ribs, which in turn pulled my shoulder blades apart and stretched my back, like a tire being over-inflated. The air rushing in made a deafening roar as it streamed through flared nostrils, past neatly trimmed and diminished turbinate structures, to where the now-correctly-positioned septum divided the flow equally between left and right passages. My sinuses were sucked bone dry through newly drilled-out orifices.

I had to learn to be more careful. A mere sniff became amplified into a full-blown gasp for air that stopped only when the elastic limit of my chest wall was reached. If I forgot and breathed in deeply my chest would surge outward and I would swell up like a frog serenading its mate at the edge of a pond. I became buoyant and light-headed—almost giddy—at the sensation. I learned to breathe cautiously, and without discernible effort. And yet I still sucked in vast quantities of oxygen—far more than I needed.

Breathing out carried with it the same kind of hazard. Anything in my nasal passages would be forcibly ejected at the slightest effort to expel air through my nostrils. I had to be extra careful not to forget and snort when in the presence of others. But at the same time I discovered an unforeseen advantage. Holding one nostril shut by placing my finger on the side of my nose, I could clear the other nostril without the need of tissues or handkerchiefs, blowing my nose the way I had seen carpenters and laborers do all my life. The nose was left clean and empty, inside and out, everything objectionable blown well away from the immediate vicinity. The practice did little to endear me to some who saw me demonstrate it.

I discovered also that my allergies were gone. No, in the interest of reasonableness, that's not quite right either. To say that would be mistaking symptom for cause. Gone were the outward symptoms of my allergies—the clogged sinuses and swollen, itchy membranes, the perpetually blocked or runny nose. Now the fresh air swirled in and out like glorious sunshine, sweeping everything clean and dry, leaving me free of symptoms for the first time in years. I feel certain I still reacted to the same allergens, only now without the same debilitating effects.

Maybe the surgery was not to blame, though that doesn't mean I hold the surgeon blameless by any means. The nose seemed to be working fine—mechanically, that is. Except now it detected the unmistakable odor of something I had never before noticed.

Years ago, when I used to smoke tobacco laced with Turkish latakia and other exotic blends of aromatic leaf—in my favorite calabash with its meerschaum bowl—I noticed a similar effect. After a few bowlfuls of Balkan Sobranie I could switch to something more harsh, like Prince Albert, only to find that it tasted the same. I could smoke a cigarette—the brand didn't matter, Camels, Marlboros, even Kools—they all tasted alike too, just like that aromatic tobacco with its Turkish latakia. A succulent, hearty taste like barbecued meat. I salivate even now thinking about it. That dry, robust, delicious aroma in which all of my youthful dreams and adventures and aspirations are forever enshrouded. It is one of the most unmistakable components of my memory, like the scent of fresh-mown grass or ripe watermelon, in precipitating the flood of memories that come rushing upon us unawares.

The aroma of that tobacco got stuck in my nose. We won't bother here with how that might have happened. To do so might be interesting enough—to us as reductionists and mechanists. I am sure we could propose a working hypothesis, build it into a plausible theory, invoke some telling observations in support of it, and, I wager, make the whole thing into a believable, even a satisfying and appealing, explanation. But in the process we would almost surely become embroiled in a pointless controversy about the merits—or should I be more fashionable and say the evils?—of smoking, and that would lead us hopelessly astray and detract from the very point I set out to make. That aroma, like the one I smelled now, simply got stuck in my nose.

Then one day the pungent aromatic odor, sharp and slightly metallic, musty even—medicinal, like something from a pharmacy or concocted in a chemistry lab—began to smell exactly like automobile exhaust fumes. Perhaps it had all along and I just finally figured out what I had been smelling. Or maybe it had slowly evolved. Or perhaps my sense of smell was improved by the surgery. Where before I could only breathe through my nose with difficulty, now I could draw copious quantities of air past my olfactory sensors, test it, and blow it out again to draw in more, sampling the aroma as often and as long and as deeply as I wished. What I detected when I did so was the unmistakable odor of automobile exhaust fumes.

Sitting in my living room in the dead of night I could smell the partly combusted residues of gasoline, petrol, naphtha—refined petroleum. In my office with the windows open, the sunlight streaming in and the fresh air cool against my face, I smelled the same distinctive odor. Indoors, outside, everywhere it was the same—the smell of automobile exhaust fumes permeated everything.

I made the mistake of confiding my discovery to some of my friends. What should I call them? Acquaintances? Confidants? Associates? Colleagues? I am not certain anymore. They were acquaintances to be sure and people in whom I had no reluctance to confide. At one time I would have called them my friends without hesitation. They were certainly people I cared about and who I believed cared about me. But when I asked them if they could not detect the subtle aroma of oxidized petroleum, they clucked and wagged their heads and quickly changed the subject.

If I had truly asked them—as I was more and more tempted to do—why they thought they too could not smell the overwhelming stench that I detected everywhere, they would have turned away in disgust and shunned me, and we would have had nothing more to say to each other. Or perhaps they were right, and the stench that I detected was only overwhelming in its subtlety.

My preoccupation with my nose began to affect my other behavior. Soon I began to read differently. Where before I had pictured in my mind images of what I was reading, now I began to imagine—to actually smell—the aromas that accompanied the images. The nativity scene, and indeed all of the Biblical story, became one of frankincense and myrrh for me. The trade routes to the orient became redolent with the wafting fragrances of rich perfumes. The ocean voyages of exploration, discovery, and conquest that opened up the new world were filled with the exciting scents of spices, tea, cocoa, coffee, tobacco, and rum. The drawing rooms of the French philosophes and encyclopedists, and the taverns of the English debating societies reeked of incense and strong spirits and the scented talc of powered wigs.

To cover up the ubiquitous odor of combusted gasoline, I took to wearing perfumed aftershave lotions and colognes, using pine-scented soaps and bath oils, and burning incense sticks and scented candles about the house and office. This however brought me no relief. It merely put me in conflict with those who demanded a fragrance-free work place, who insisted on their right to be free of any offending odors from my person. When I inquired whether they were not equally offended by the irritating smell of exhaust fumes all about them—by the smell of the world itself—they looked at me as if I had gone mad.

Even with the burning incense, sweet-smelling aftershave lotions and perfumed colognes I could still smell the pervasive odor of exhaust fumes. I had discovered that every age has its own distinctive aroma. That I could not cover up the smell of dung and straw and animals with frankincense and myrrh. Or mask the odor of sweat and unwashed bodies, or rotting meat and raw sewage, with perfumes and spices, or with tobacco and rum. That the acrid smell of burning wood and soft peat, and the mustiness of mold, mud and dank cold, could penetrate the fragrance of incense and perfumed talc and exciting new ideas. That what truly characterizes an age is not its commerce, its fashions or its ideas, but how it smells. And what counts is how it smells when we take away all of the trappings and really smell it, for the first time.

I am reassured to discover since then that I have not become paranoid or exhibited other obvious manifestations of psychosis. Apparently my olfactory sensations were not the early symptoms of some progressive and more serious form of dementia—unless you could call just being alive a kind of dementia. I have not become overly suspicious. Nor do I feel threatened, or imagine that I am the subject of some elaborate and carefully executed conspiracy to drive me over the brink and deprive me of my sanity. I am not the object of some diabolical plot, either at the hands of others or as the result of circumstances. I just know what I smell. I can identify the odor of exhaust fumes when I detect them. And let me assure you, I smell them everywhere these days.

My friends have gradually gotten used to my little preoccupations. They no longer find it strange or alarming whenever I ask them—in their living rooms or offices—whether they smell exhaust fumes. They have stopped clucking and wagging their heads and trying to change the subject, though I suspect they still grow impatient with me. Occasionally I even wear a coat and tie, though I do not now put a cloth noose about my neck simply for the sake of decorum or convention. And I much prefer comfortable footwear over formality. I find songs with lyrics that say something much more interesting and appealing than pleasing musical harmony. It is even better if the singer writes his own material. Better still if one can be assured that the song has actually been lived, and not just made up to try and fool someone.

I suppose I still imagine at times that something is wrong. But if so, no one has been able to figure it out or explain it to me in any way that is satisfying or convincing. In fact, it seems less and less necessary to explain it at all. Probably there is nothing wrong with my nose. Nothing, that is, except that it tells me the truth. I may simply have the curious fortune to be able to smell the true nature of our age. I am even beginning to think it may not be so bad, once you get used to it. There does seem to be a danger though. Now that I have grown almost accustomed to the way things smell, I too may cease to notice it in time.

PRACTICING MEDICINE

"What seems to be the matter sweetheart?"

A pleasant-faced nurse in white stockings bent over the crying child. She smiled and brushed the tears off the little girl's cheek.

"It's her arm," the man said. "She fell out of a swing and landed hard on it. I didn't want to bring her in but she cries every time I touch it or try to move it. I was afraid it could be broken." The girl held her left arm clamped tightly against her side with her other hand.

"Let me see it sweetheart," the nurse said. She cradled the girl's forearm gingerly in one hand and with her other hand carefully rotated the wrist on the injured arm, first in one direction then the other. The little girl resumed her screaming.

"Let the nurse take a look at it, Lydia," the man said. "She's going to make it better." The girl closed her eyes and cried all the harder. "That's what she does every time I try to touch it," the man said. "She can move her fingers."

"We'll have to take some X-rays," the nurse said. She turned and left the small examining room.

The emergency ward of the hospital was crowded. On a Sunday afternoon the man hadn't known where else to take the injured child. Angela would have known what to do if she had been there, he thought. He didn't think the arm was broken, but he didn't feel comfortable deciding that on his own and he didn't know how else to explain the way she screamed every time he tried to examine it. The nurse had ushered them into the small examining room away from the reception area, to separate the screaming child from the other patients crowded into the waiting room and along the corridors of the emergency suite.

When the nurse stepped out of the room, the girl quieted and sat holding her arm against her side, crying less now. Soon the nurse returned with a wheel chair, coaxed the girl into it and pushed her out of the room and down the hall to the elevators where, he presumed, she would be taken to the radiology department or wherever it was that X-rays were made.

The prospect of riding in a wheelchair instantly quieted the girl and for the first time since her fall she became interested in something besides her injured arm. She even rested it on the padded arm of the chair instead of holding it clamped against her side, and he saw her looking at the people on either side of her as the nurse pushed the wheelchair down the crowded hallway.

The elevator doors closed and the man stood and watched the red arrow indicating down light up on the wall beside the closed doors. He presumed that the nurse would have motioned to him if he was supposed to accompany them. He made his way back along the hallway toward the examining room. He went past the examining room to the reception desk where he had been when the nurse interrupted him, and now he completed the questionnaire that the receptionist handed him when he first checked in. He signed the completed form and gave it to the woman behind the counter.

"Who is your pediatrician?" she asked him.

"We don't have one. We're new here."

"No orthopedic specialist?"

"No," he said.

"I'll see who is on call today," she told him.

He didn't want to wait cooped up in the cramped examining room where he couldn't see anything or tell what was going on around him. There were no empty seats in the reception area, so for a time he paced slowly back and forth, looking about and peering with interest into the various rooms along the crowded corridors until he began to feel conspicuous and out of place and he stood to one side along a portion of the hallway that was unoccupied by chairs or gurneys. Opposite him, mounted on the wall, was a row of light boxes, the kind used to backlight and display medical X-rays, and it was for that reason that this particular portion of the hallway had been left unobstructed and uncluttered.

He found himself wondering if all these people could possibly be patients. Only a portion of them are here for medical attention he told himself. The others are family members or friends who brought them or who came along to accompany them. He stood thinking about this as he studied the people crowded into the waiting room and along the hallways. None of them appeared seriously ill or injured. They must treat the true emergencies first, he thought. What had he expected? Stabbings, gunshot wounds, broken bones, heart attacks? At least someone bleeding or unconscious. Wasn't it always depicted like that? These people sat quietly and stared dully ahead or downward at nothing in particular. Occasionally one of them would speak to the person sitting alongside before lapsing back into silence and waiting. To him they seemed strangely passive and lethargic. Not at all the way he imagined an emergency room. The only movement was that of the nurses and one or two doctors in white frocks worn over street clothes who went methodically about their business.

A name would be called and that person would be ushered away by a nurse to one of the examining rooms along the hallway or to one of the treatment areas curtained off for privacy. He watched as one of the two doctors he had identified made his rounds between the rooms along the corridor, never getting in a hurry and never lingering anywhere for very long. They are all here like me, he told himself. Where else, if you are sick and need to see a doctor on a Sunday afternoon, would you go? The only real emergency is that it's Sunday, he thought.

"Mr. Harris, please check with the receptionist at the desk." The voice came over the public address system from speakers he couldn't see. He gradually became aware that it was his name the voice was speaking. He answered a few more questions, then read over the completed and typed forms the receptionist handed him, and signed them in all the places she had marked.

"Everything seems to be in order," she said.

As he walked back to his place along the corridor he saw the elevator doors open and Lydia emerged, being pushed in the wheelchair by a technician who wore a white smock with "RADIOLOGY" stamped in faded black letters above the pocket. Lydia was not crying anymore. She was carrying a Dr. Seuss book, Green Eggs and Ham, that someone had given her.

"The doctor has examined her," the nurse told him. "He'll be in to see her once the X-rays are available."

With that she left the room and he followed her out into the hall and quietly pulled the door shut. Lydia was engrossed in looking at the book and he didn't want to take a chance on breaking the spell and upsetting her again.

As he waited in the corridor he noticed someone he had not seen earlier, a tall imposing man in a tan Western suit wearing an expensive felt Stetson and hand tooled cowboy boots and smoking a long black cigar. Around his neck he wore a silver bolo inlaid in the center with an enormous chunk of Kingman turquoise. He was dressed like a rich Texas oilman or New Mexico rancher, and he seemed oddly out of place among all the other people in the emergency suite. The man's appearance, like something right out of Neiman Marcus, was enough to call attention to him, but his manner too set him apart. He alternately stood or slowly paced, almost stalking, his left arm folded across his chest and grasping the upper part of his right arm, his right forearm and fingers holding the cigar up to his mouth. He looked straight ahead seemingly at nothing in particular, as though in deep thought, and from time to time he absentmindedly puffed copious clouds of smoke from his cigar. The hospital staff paid him no attention and scurried past him. He spoke to no one and he seemed oblivious to everything going on around him.

While Ian Harris was occupied studying the man, a technician came by and put two large X-rays up on the light box. He could see the name LYDIA HARRIS in bright block letters at the top of each one and he moved over to examine them closer. He noticed at once the crisp clear contrast between the light and dark portions of the images on the film. Over-exposed and under-developed—the thought came instantly to his mind. The surest way to get a good image. Carl Compton had taught him that.

He remembered the X-ray on the wall of the physics department at the university. William Kennedy had made it shortly after X-rays were discovered by Roentgen. "Wild Bill" his students called him because of his fiery red hair and flamboyant manner. Ever the showman, Kennedy had immediately made his own x-ray tube shortly after first reading about Roentgen's work, and he was soon demonstrating the uses of its peculiar penetrating radiation to his students. The football players all took his astronomy class to satisfy their physical science requirement. One of them happened to injure his finger during a scrimmage, and to find out what was wrong with it Wild Bill made an X-ray of the injured hand. A clean fracture of the middle digit of his ring finger separating the bone into two pieces was clearly visible in the X-ray, along with the bright image of the ring that could not be removed from the swollen finger and an outline of the bones in his hand and wrist.

My God, what a dose he must have given him, he thought, probably tens of roentgens. His hand might have gotten even more. It's a wonder Kennedy didn't kill himself, or injure someone; but he didn't so far as anyone knew. He had gone on to train two of Ian

Harris's teachers and was chairman of the physics department for nearly fifty years before he retired, still proud of the X-ray of that young man's hand that he had kept all those years on the wall of his office. When he, Ian Harris, remarked about the sharpness of the image, Dr. Callen explained that the film had probably been overexposed to guarantee a useful image on the first attempt. Any good x-ray technician learned about that trick. Standing there looking at the X-ray of Lydia's arm, and remembering, he thought to himself, well, at least Carl Compton had tried to change all that.

"Do you see anything wrong with that arm?"

The voice startled him. He turned to find the man in the tan suit standing beside him, the cigar clamped between two outstretched fingers of his right hand still held up in front of his face.

"I'm sorry, are you talking to me?"

"Do you see anything wrong with that arm?" The man repeated the question, not glancing to either side but looking directly ahead, as though talking mainly to himself. Ian Harris was still not sure the voice was speaking to him. There was no one else nearby.

"I really don't know a thing about it," he finally blurted out. "Reading medical X-rays, I mean."

"Well, I'm no radiologist either, but I swear I can't see a thing wrong with that arm. Looks like an X-ray of a perfectly normal arm to me." He looked neither left nor right, not at Ian Harris or at anything around him, but stared straight ahead at the two pieces of film displayed on the light box in front of him. As he continued to study the film he put the cigar in his mouth and slowly expelled a dense cloud of whitish smoke. The dissipating cloud reminded Ian Harris of the way the images on the X-ray faded to a gray haziness at the edges.

Do you suppose he has any idea that I'm Lydia's father, he wondered to himself. How could he, he thought. Maybe he had just assumed it. He considered whether to say anything about it. While he was considering it the man spoke again, still staring only at the X-ray in front of him but now including Ian Harris in what he said.

"The trouble is she complains of severe pain whenever I move the arm. And the pain seems to be real." He paused again as if he had slipped back into thought. "I'll tell you what we could do. She doesn't complain of pain in the other arm. We could take her back down to radiology and take a picture of the good arm and compare the two X-rays. If we can't see any difference in them, then I don't think we need to do anything more." Then after a short pause, "What do you think?"

He didn't know what to say. My God, that sounds like something I might think of, he told himself. Is he really serious? Is he asking my permission? I don't think so; I think he's just talking to himself. He turned to find the man walking away, toward the nurse's station where he stopped briefly and spoke to the pleasant-faced nurse in white stockings who had attended Lydia.

He stayed there examining the X-rays, looking at every feature of both views, one from the front of the arm, the other from the back. He could see both bones of the forearm, the radius and the ulna, plus the bones of the wrist and part of the hand. He still remembered the names from high school biology class. Maybe a view from the side would have shown something different he thought. After thinking about it for a while he finally dismissed the idea. It wouldn't have added anything he realized. He could see why they took the two views they did, to examine each side of both bones in the forearm plus the small bones in the upper wrist. He couldn't discern anything in the images that even suggested a fracture, and the images were too indistinct to make out anything but the bones. He knew that the fainter shadows in the less distinct portions of the X-ray might mean something to a radiologist trained to look for it, but to him they were just an unintelligible blur. He could plainly see the fractured finger in the X-ray on the wall of the physics department, but then anyone could see that with no training.

He looked away from the X-rays just in time to see Lydia being wheeled once more into the elevator by the same technician who had brought her back the first time. She still had the book with her and she seemed content now. He watched as the doors closed and the red arrow indicating down lit up. He wondered if he should have objected. He knew the machines were much better and safer now, the film more sensitive and the radiation dose required to make a high-quality X-ray was only a small fraction of what it had been in the past. The suggestion to compare the two arms appealed to the experimenter in him. It seemed so simple, so direct, so commonsensical and practical—and so refreshing. It was an approach that anyone could understand and appreciate. There was about it a kind of simple elegance, the kind of elegance that had always made physics and mathematics appeal to him. Still he wondered what Carl Compton would have said. His teacher had always stressed the need to avoid any unnecessary radiation exposure, especially for females who already carried inside them all of the eggs they would ever produce, each one potentially an unborn child. In a long career Carl Compton had seen too much ignorance and too many abuses to trust anyone who used radiation. He certainly felt no reverence for MDs.

Lydia was gone much longer this time. When she returned she was accompanied by the pleasant-faced nurse in white stockings. Lydia no longer had the book but she was smiling now and talking with the nurse. Someone had put her arm in a cloth sling that hung around her neck.

"The doctor examined her again," the nurse told him. "He said that he couldn't find any difference between the two arms and didn't feel any need to go further. He thought you would understand. He said to let her use it and to just keep an eye on it for a few days."

She leaned over toward him and whispered in his ear, "The sling was my idea. It wasn't really necessary, but I thought it might make her feel better." He thought her hair smelled nice. When she drew away she smiled at him and winked and he noticed that she was pretty. She accompanied them to the door still pushing Lydia in the wheel chair. As she turned to go she smiled and said, "I hope to see you again, but without an injured arm next time." She looked knowingly at him. He should have known what Lydia would tell her.

"Wait," he said. "Who was the doctor?"

"Oh," she laughed, "that was Dr. Sforza, William Sforza. He's an orthopedic surgeon. He happened to be the one on call today. I'm sure you must have noticed, he's quite a colorful character. We call him Wild Bill behind his back." She looked at him and smiled. "Don't worry. He's a very good doctor."

A STORY OF THREE PARABLES

A man wished to live forever. He did not desire this out of any sense of purpose or because of deep convictions about the meaning of life, but for entirely selfish reasons. He was not living to comfort an aging mother or to care for a wife and children, for he had none, or to fulfill an obligation to society, but merely for himself. He simply wished to live as long as he could. The whole purpose of his life was wrapped up in that one wish.

He was an intelligent man. He was trained for life in the fashion that passes for an education, and knowledgeable about the so-called facts of his existence, which he kept up with mostly by reading the newspapers and following public affairs on television. He had a number of friends and practiced a profession that enabled him to live comfortably in a tolerant and affluent society.

He was very much attuned to the times. He avoided everything he thought might pose some threat, however slight, to his desire to live a long life. He had been addicted to tobacco at a young age, the result of a nervous and aggressive disposition, but as opinions hardened and he found that it was a habit he could not practice in moderation, he gave it up entirely. He early found himself partial to alcohol, and although not an alcoholic, he enjoyed the release from his normal inhibitions that accompanied its use and he drank to excess. Only under the influence of alcohol was he capable of believing that, given the right circumstances, he might be creative. With time, increasing amounts of alcohol were required to drown his inhibitions. He attempted to control his drinking, at first by eliminating hard liquor and limiting himself to fine wines at meals. He discovered however that it was not the wines but the alcohol that he desired, and afterwards he abstained totally.

Like everyone young he experimented with sex, even imagining at one time that he was attracted not just to members of the opposite sex. Under the constant barrage of warnings however he gave that up too. He did not feel inclined to intimacy with only one person, and found himself at first mildly amused and then later put off by the idea of practicing safe sex, a notion that struck him as strangely at odds with the mystery and the sense of excitement and danger that he had experienced during his own sexual gropings. Still, he did not wish to die from the indiscretions of others, so he did what he felt was necessary and became celibate.

He used his training and his knowledge to steer clear of risks. He ate the right foods, avoided too much fat and cholesterol, included fiber and carotenes in his diet, and curtailed his intake of red meat. He took vitamin and mineral supplements and kept up with the latest health food trends. He followed the recommendations of herbal medicine, picking and choosing those that seemed to have some substantiated efficacy or that at least had demonstrated no deleterious effects. He was especially enamored of regimens and dietary supplements that purported to boost and strengthen the immune system. He avoided doctors, in particular surgeons and those practicing any kind of invasive therapy. He became something of an expert on natural healing and naturopathy; and in his reading was especially drawn to those how-to manuals that included specific chapters on how-not-to when it came to encountering any of the major killers. He exercised regularly, but only in deliberate moderation, and was careful to get plenty of rest. To relieve stress and anxiety he practiced yoga, read Eastern philosophy, and meditated. Yet he was by no means a caricature, merely an ordinary man, one in equilibrium and harmony with his surroundings.

Then at a relatively young age, even before what one could call middle age, the man discovered that he was going to die. The reasons had nothing to do with the way he had lived. They were merely the workings of fate, an accident of genetics, nothing that anyone could have prevented, and at this point irreversible. His time was measured at most in months, yet long enough for him to feel regret.

At first he felt cheated that he had lived when the state of knowledge was only sufficient to inform him of a doom from which it could do nothing to shield him. He knew enough to realize that his condition was one that in time would be curable, if not eliminated outright. He felt resentment at being a victim of the times. But that feeling brought him no solace and little satisfaction. He turned instead to finding who or what was at fault. Those who stood in the way of progress suddenly seemed to him small-minded and mean-spirited, hypocrites of the very advances in human affairs that allowed them to oppose what they themselves had used to full advantage. He blamed them for his condition without being able to say how they had caused it. Even if they were not directly at fault, he reasoned, they represented an attitude bereft of all hope. He grew to despise them and to hold them in contempt. At length he even came to hate them, without ever knowing a single one of those whom he so loathed.

But this anger was too abstract and superficial to afford him any satisfaction. It soon gave way to a deeper, more profound anger, one that grew out of his bitterness toward himself. He felt betrayed that he had denied himself the sensual pleasures of life, or even the experiences that would have let him decide if it was truly those pleasures that he desired. His friends tried to console him with the thought that he had instead lived a life of discipline and purpose and virtue. Their attempts only hardened his bitterness. In his heart he knew the truth. Discipline perhaps, but there had been no lofty purpose behind his denial, only the blind compelling urge to go on living. He was inconsolable. Their virtue sat like a stone on his heart, crushing the life out of him.

What he desired now, and regretted most bitterly, were the lost opportunities, the succulent foods, the gratification of strong drink, the company of compliant women that he might have made love to. He missed especially – or imagined that he did – the private pleasures of lust and the sweet exhilaration of falling in love. He could recall the way he had felt each time he found himself attracted to a desirable woman, only to deny himself the fulfillment. If he could do it all over, he would fall in love again and again. He would try to be always in love, to enjoy the tingling excitement and the sweet anticipation of as many lovers as possible. In this he was mindful not of others but only of himself at his impending death. He gave no thought to any disappointment or betrayal but his own. Discipline and virtue struck him as hollow slogans spoken by those who have settled for them as all that life can hold. He would not subscribe to consolations that he disdained as false and alien. Only by an unhappy death and the gratification of his bitterness and anger could he approach any measure of satisfaction. At the end, he refused all painkilling medication.

Another man lived a long and indulgent life. In his youth he was noted for his profligate behavior. Even in his advancing years he continued to be consumed by the pleasures of the flesh. Throughout his life he denied himself nothing, abusing his body, indiscreetly pursuing many lovers, and callously taking advantage of his friends and family.

He was this way by nature from the very beginning. He had been a handsome youth with fine sensual features and he had relieved several young girls of their virginity almost before the age when they first realized it was something that could be lost. In turn he willingly allowed himself to be seduced by a number of older women who opened his eyes to the possibilities and whetted his appetite for greater sexual gratification. He made a practice of every vice. From a young age he used tobacco, experimented with drugs, and drank heavily. In everything he craved the excitement of his indiscretions and openly courted danger. It was only through his fortunate social circumstances, the occasional intervention of his family, and his inordinate good luck that he escaped any serious altercation with authority and was able to continue to live free in society.

Yet he was also intelligent and his experiences taught him to be resourceful and self-reliant. He learned to fend for himself, to live by his wits and to take advantage of the many opportunities that society offered. He possessed a natural charm and the keen insight into human nature that allowed him to manipulate and control others to his special advantage. In a word, he became successful. Others tolerated his licentious manner and looked past the indulgent behavior, beguiled by his success and charm and content with whatever benefit they derived from their association with him.

Though he could not—or at least would not—deny himself the pleasures that his lustful nature craved, he lived always with an inner dread of the consequences and in perpetual fear that he would die young, wasted and spent by a life of dissipation. This premonition had been strongest in his youth and took the form of a conviction that he would never reach manhood, or that if he did he would do so only to live a life of impairment brought on by his indiscretions. As he grew older this fear was replaced by one that he would die before accomplishing whatever purpose his life was intended to fulfill, perhaps even before he had come to realize what that purpose might be. In later years this fear shifted to a dread that he would die a terrible and painful death resulting from the abuse of his body. His fears mocked him constantly in feelings of guilt and shame and self-loathing.

Then as he passed middle age and grew older, he gradually

realized that he was meant to live a long time. He understood also that his longevity was merely an accident, the workings of circumstance, not anything that he deserved but something granted by nothing more profound than the simple way the world is. The world is indifferent, and out of that indifference he was destined to live a long life. As a result of pure whim he would escape what he had dreaded most, the fate of dying too soon, consumed by the pleasures he could not deny or resist.

By then however, it was too late. He did not find joy in the realization that he would not soon die. Nor did he derive greater pleasure as a result from his indulgences. Instead he became increasingly bitter at the years squandered in feelings of guilt and shame. He suddenly realized that he had never truly enjoyed himself because of the fear and uncertainty that he would be punished for his licentiousness by an early death. Now that that prospect was removed he felt cheated out of his best years which might have been spent in even greater pleasure. For him the years became more and more a mockery, a punishment devoid of the pleasure he had spent his life pursuing but was now becoming too old to enjoy. Food, drink, sex lost their savor. Too often he found himself dwelling on his regrets rather than enjoying the experience of the moment.

When his friends tried to console him by speaking about the need to find inner peace and achieve some final dignity, he scoffed at them. When they spoke about the need for discipline and responsibility—for the triumph of virtue—he became openly hostile. Your virtue has made my life an agony of mental torment, he bellowed at them. He was inconsolable in his scorn. He would not be cheated out of the pleasure of his final fury, and died in a final rage.

A third man also lived a life of wantonness and consumption. He too denied himself nothing—food, drink, the pleasures of sex. His life was a continuous quest to gratify his senses in an orgy of gluttony and carnal lust. He did so without qualms about the consequences or concern for the future. He was without remorse or guilt or apology for his behavior.

Then at a young age he learned that his pleasures had cost him his life, that he would soon die. His death was clearly the result of the choices he had made about how he would live. He had no one to blame but himself and his own bad luck.

Still, he became bitter. Not at himself for how he had lived, but at the world, at the prospect of a life of pleasure cut short, at what he felt was the taunting injustice of being denied more time to indulge himself. He thought not of those who cared for him, for whom his death would be a traumatic loss and a real hardship, but only of himself and his own desires. He felt betrayed and angry at the loss of the pleasures that were the only thing he had lived for, the only thing that had made life worthwhile. Even at the end, when he might have prolonged his life for a while through abstinence and moderation, he refused to renounce the behavior that was hastening his death. He was inconsolable. He died unappeased and bitterly disappointed.

A fourth man had a long and distinguished life of moderation and virtue, a life of the mind with the intellect firmly in control of the passions and emotions. His greatest pleasures were those of contemplation and reflection. He possessed the magnanimity of spirit and evenness of intellect that one associates with philosophy. Throughout his life he devoted himself to serving others in whatever way he could. He always elevated the needs and the greater good of society above his own interests. He was revered by his friends, respected by his colleagues, and held in esteem by all who knew him. Near the end of his life he learned the story of these other three men. At the time of his own death, he confided to his friends that he could find no fault with any of them.

A CERTAIN FEELING

He saw death for the first time seven summers ago. He was by himself then and had lots of time on his hands. That morning he had made his way through a freshly mown field to the edge of a narrow stream that meandered in tight loops back and forth across the valley. The pungent fragrance of wild mint growing along the stream bank hung in the warm stagnant air. The sky was everywhere a deep bottomless blue except where the brilliant white light of the sun overwhelmed and obscured it. When he reached the stream he eased into the shallow water beside a low grassy bank. He turned upstream to face the current and made a short lazy cast, flipping the line lightly in front of him. And as he watched the hackled fly settle upright onto the smooth surface of the water, he saw death for the first time. Not in any distinct, tangible form, but in the same way he had known when he got up that morning, by the peculiar slant of light and a certain feeling in the air, that the seasons had shifted and it was suddenly autumn.

He watched the fly drift and turn on the slow steady current. As it drew even with him in the stream, he felt death drift by. Then a big brown trout rose in one smooth easy motion and sucked in the fly, and the feeling passed as quickly as it had come over him. Now seven years later, death was that much closer, and he saw it everywhere. He could feel its presence, not constant, but never far from anything he thought or did. He had grown accustomed to it, and it did not bother him.

Something had gone out of him that summer. Some intensity or passion that he had not been aware of until it was no longer there. He felt tired and he had to force himself to do the things he had always enjoyed and looked forward to before. It was not a physical tiredness but a kind of vague weariness that went much deeper. Whenever he began anything he found himself asking why he should want to continue it. He had done enough. He had fished and hunted enough, traveled enough, seen enough, and thought enough. None of it seemed to satisfy him anymore. He told himself he was just bored and that it would pass. In time it did pass, and he found the desire to continue, but it was not the same as before. Now death was seven years closer, and he knew he was finally running out of time.

Where had the time gone, he asked himself? He had spent it, some of it wisely, some of it foolishly. He had no regrets about any of it, only a mild, curious surprise that it seemed to have gone by so quickly. All of it had been the result of trying to make some sense out of the world. That, he thought, had been his true life's work. Making sense out of the world. There was nothing remarkable in that. He supposed it was really the life's work of everyone who lived—to make sense out of the world in some fashion. What else is there, he thought? In the end it all came down to how one chose to make sense out of things.

In retrospect, he admitted, he had squandered too much of it on the narrow pursuit of science. Life held consequences for the choices he had made. After an active youth he made a conscious decision to pursue a life devoted to thought rather than a life of action. Early on he had been drawn to ideas and knowledge, and he had set aside other pursuits to follow a path of learning and contemplation. He turned to science for the understanding he sought and devoted years trying to make sense out of the world that way. Now everything he thought he once understood seemed in danger of being undermined. With each new discovery all of it seemed destined to change. Nothing, not even in science, could ever be certain. Nothing except mathematics, and that was a game he lost interest in a long time ago.

That realization was the only certainty he had gained from the years devoted to science, and it was, he knew now, the only truth one ever got from trying to understand what was beyond understanding. He had enjoyed the pursuit for a while but he had learned enough to see through the false hopes he had entertained when he set out, and he did not want to spend more time going down that path. He was comfortable with what he knew, and comfortable also with the things yet to be discovered that he didn't know, which in their turn would give way to still different views. He no longer felt driven to keep up with each new discovery or revelation, except as a kind of reminder or confirmation of his feeling that he was right. He was confident that whatever came out of it he would be able to incorporate somehow into his understanding of the world. The same way that he imagined someone in the middle ages must have done. That was perhaps the one sure thing he had learned.

When he was younger he had envisioned spending the last years of his life thinking about what he knew and making some final sense out of it all before he died. He had always thought that was what Plato and Aristotle had in mind as the philosopher's ultimate reward. An immortality devoted to contemplation. Not to discovering the truth, but to thinking back upon those truths already acquired during a lifetime of questioning and thinking. Now it seemed to him only a pointless waste of time. He could face death without having to be reassured about what he knew.

He didn't feel compelled either to substitute a life of action for one of contemplation, to try to fend off the inevitable by attempting to squeeze in everything he had sacrificed in the pursuit of knowledge. He confessed to a small regret earlier when he first realized how fast life was going by, and how much he had given up in the years devoted to science. He appeased his regret by indulging for a time in some of those other pursuits he had set aside, and it, too, soon passed.

Along the way he had managed to get some things right. He had never done anything merely for money. He had never had money, but he hadn't desired it either and he had never felt deprived of anything he truly needed or wanted. When it came his way he didn't turn his back on it and he had always tried to use what little he had well. But to live life in the pursuit of money he considered the biggest waste of all. He was not in awe of those who had money either. He had known his share of them. They were like anyone else as far as he could tell. Some of them he liked and admired but not because of their money. Those who took money as a sign of their superior ability or special status, or who believed that the rich had a responsibility or a right to be in charge of things, he distrusted most of all. Those he opposed in any way he could. The worst and most insufferable were the ones who thought their success was somehow their own doing, the result of talent and hard work. For those he felt only contempt and pity, for they remained ignorant of their own good luck.

He hadn't committed the terrible sin of his forefathers either. He had never allowed himself to think he was better than other men. "You gotta make sump'n o' yo'self," the old Negro used to tell him, the tobacco stained teeth showing through his smile. He lived in a dilapidated shack behind the Methodist church across the street. Once it had been a carriage house, long ago in the days of slavery. After the

War it was converted into living quarters for some freed slave who moved to town and became a house servant, choosing to work for no wages beyond food and housing and discarded clothing, when the only alternative was to stay on the depleted and ravaged and forsaken land and starve as a sharecropper. The old Negro watched after him on those evenings when his parents went out. He would bring his briar pipe with its round bowl oiled and polished smooth by years of cradling and fondling it in his hands, its stem grooved and chipped where his teeth had held it; and the boy's father would give him tobacco and the old black man would contentedly puff great clouds of blue smoke that to the boy smelled of men and leather and the outdoors. He would climb up in the old man's lap and listen as the soft, low voice told him stories about the old days. He could still recall the smell of the old Negro, stale and musty like soiled cotton flannel. He liked to run his hand over the old man's head and feel the gray cottony nap that fringed the balding pate. He could still feel too the rough brown skin on his hands and arms that had always reminded him of parched and cracked earth when he touched it.

No matter what stories he told, there was always some moral or point to them by which he would remind the boy, "You gotta make sump'n o' yo'self." When he said it the rheumy, bloodshot eyes held a distant far away look as if seeing something the boy could not. The longing that he had seen in the old man's eyes was what he remembered most. His old shack burned down one night. The boy's mother saved his life, they said, pounding on the door to wake him. A pot of water on the stove boiled dry and melted. He was almost blind. After that he never saw him much. He guessed he finally just got too old. But he never forgot him either, or the kind patient face and the wisdom and longing he saw in his eyes.

He thought too of Mrs. Rafferty who lived down the street. She was widowed and lived alone in a white house with green trim. On warm days in the spring and fall he would see her sitting on the front porch as he walked to and from school. For some reason she took a special interest in him and would call him over to come up on the porch where she could talk to him. She asked him how he was doing in school and she encouraged him and gave him advice. One thing in particular he recalled. She always told him how important she considered good penmanship. "Whatever you do, learn to write a beautiful hand," she said. "Good handwriting is a mark of distinction for a gentleman." It was a curious thing, he knew, but it made a deep and lasting impression on him. He practiced his writing for hours, carefully printing the letters of the alphabet to neatly fill the spaces between the lines in his writing tablet, both capitals and lower-case letters, striving to make each one as nearly like those in his writing manual as he could. He did the same with the cursive letters when he learned them.

But no matter how long he practiced or how hard he tried, he did not learn to write a beautiful hand. His writing was legible but not attractive or artistic. As he progressed he sacrificed perfection of form for the greater utility of speed, and his script became a tiny almost illegible scrawl in the effort to have his writing keep pace with his thoughts. Even then he remembered Mrs. Rafferty's words. To make his handwriting more legible he adopted a tiny script that was a mixture of printing and cursive, yet even so he fell miserably short of the goal Mrs. Rafferty had set for him. Still he guessed he owed to her something of his passion for good writing and his constant striving to write well himself.

Years later he went to visit her. He had in mind thanking her after all those years for her kind interest in the young boy who had walked past her house each day on the way to and from school, and for her influence on his life and success. He found her sitting on her porch, older now, her fine steel-gray hair done up in a fashionable bun on top of her head. The house, unchanged and well kept, seemed somehow more modest and less prepossessing than he remembered it.

Mrs. Rafferty did not remember him, or the advice she had once given him. When he brought it up she seized on the chance to talk about what she saw happening around her. "It's all the niggers' fault," she said. "Especially the young ones, wanting what is not theirs, having no respect for their betters or for the law and authority. They should stay in their place and leave us alone. We don't want to associate with niggers. I don't know what it's coming to, where it will all lead." She grew animated and venomous. He made some small attempt to reassure her. "You're not like them now, are you?" she asked him. He attempted nothing more, but wished her well and took his leave.

He thought again of the old Negro who used to sit him on his lap and tell him stories. He had never thought about him being black until much later. And he never did have a chance to find out if it mattered to the old man that he was not. He knew now what he had known then. That he loved the old Negro man, or at least his memory of him. And perhaps that was enough.

Thinking of him again he recalled another old Negro man who had come into the grocery store one Saturday morning where he had a job sweeping and oiling the wooden floors. It was the first job he ever had. The grocery store was on Main Street next door to the bank with its brown brick front and prominent clock that reached above the street. The old Negro had a personal check he was trying to cash. He sought out the owner of the store. "Mr. Ashland, sir," he said, "Mr. Castleman at the bank say he'd be willin' to cash this check if you'd endorse it for me." Nick Castleman was the president and owner of the bank. Mr. Ashland took the check and appeared to be studying it. It was for a small amount.

"Sam," he said. The Negro man was a regular customer. "This check is not written on Mr. Castleman's bank."

"No, sir, it's on the Planter's Bank in Ruleville. But I knows the man who wrote it. He's a white man. He owes me that money. Mr. Ashland, sir, I needs the money and I got no way to go to Ruleville. Can't you help me out?"

Mr. Ashland thought a bit more then looked up. "Tell you what I'll do, Sam. You take this check back over to the bank and tell Mr. Castleman that if he'll endorse it, I'll cash it." The old Negro man wandered out of the store and shuffled on down the street, squeezed between a world he could not escape and one he could never be part of. The boy never saw him again or learned what happened to him.

He had seen the young black faces around him as was growing up. Sullen and resigned, hardened and older than their years, in those unguarded moments when they did not know anyone was looking. They had not been his companions nor he theirs, but he and they each lived in worlds defined by the other. The clear steady brown eyes that peered curiously at him from the fringes of his play became, as they grew older, downcast and furtive and submissive. But he knew too they were desperate eyes. That they masked souls that would not forever accept defeat and humiliation and hopelessness. That they would at last be lifted up, to demand, and seize too if need be, what was rightfully theirs and had been too long denied them. Only then would the terrible sin of his forefathers finally be faced. He knew he couldn't escape it or avoid others caught up in its grip. But he vowed never to consider himself better than other men on that account.

He managed too to steer clear of the superstitions of his forefathers. He wanted to think for himself. He could face death with the knowledge that neither he nor anyone could ever hope to understand what it all meant. He preferred that to the God of his forefathers. The God of the Old Testament, stern and unrelenting, a dark gloomy God, wrathful and vengeful, demanding obedience, meting out punishment mercilessly on all alike. Offering nothing in return, no solace, no understanding, like a harsh vindictive parent devoid of compassion and undeserving of respect. Too much like the land he grew up in and escaped from. He could do without that kind of God. Or any other God that humans could comprehend. He could respect the unknown without fearing it, because fearing the unknown is merely foolish, and because it is unknowable and deserves our respect, but not our fear. In Sunday school they had tried to teach him about a different kind of God, a loving God of compassion and forgiveness. That God seemed to him at the time no more part of his world than of that pitiful old Negro's with his worthless check.

He had liked the stories though, because they were interesting stories not because they were about God. And because they had been his first real encounter with serious questions about the world. A preacher of the Church of Christ came to town about that time. Peter Akins had been called by God and ordained by the church to go forth and preach the gospel. He was young and handsome and brilliant and a gifted speaker with degrees in theology from the seminary. He was the closest thing to an intellectual that the boy had known. And he was married to a beautiful woman with long blond hair and a warm smile and riveting blue eyes that seemed to the boy like a shining piece of the spring sky after an April shower.

Peter Akins' sermons were polished and dazzling orations. He told the biblical stories and revealed their hidden meanings. He interpreted the scriptures, searching them with the aid of scholarly commentaries to extract the deeper truths buried in each obscure passage. He exuded confidence and certainty and great optimism about the soul and its immortality. One Sunday in each month he preached a special sermon consisting entirely of passages of scripture quoted verbatim from memory out of the King James Bible and strung together to reveal the pattern of God's divine plan for man's redemption and salvation from the eternal fires and damnation of hell. He quoted book, chapter and verse for those in the audience who wished to follow along in their Bibles. He went on for the better part of an hour with no notes, each quote memorized flawlessly and fitted neatly into its place in the unfolding story, as if Paul of Tarsus were explaining it to the Ephesians or the Corinthians. To the boy it was a stunning and impressive demonstration of learning and mental prowess like nothing he had encountered before. He imagined that this must be what was taught in seminary. The boy always attended these special sermons. He found the performance inspiring, even heroic, and he made up his mind that he too would aspire to such feats of learning. He liked the stories, and most of all he liked the search to find meaning in them. He was drawn to the ideas, and to thinking about them, not the least because he could not bring himself to believe most of them and he could always find flaws in them and reasons for doubting whether they were true, and he grew in his confidence at being able to think seriously about what interested him.

Peter Akins collected enough money in the Sunday offerings during his first year to build his congregation a new church, a handsome brick building with white Doric columns like a neoclassical Greek temple. In it he preached a series of sermons on Paul's letters to the Romans, the Corinthians and the Ephesians, taking as his text for one sermon, II Corinthians 9.6,7: "But this I say, He which soweth sparingly shall reap also sparingly; and he which soweth bountifully shall reap also bountifully. Every man according as he purposeth in his heart, so let him give; not grudgingly, or of necessity: for God loveth a cheerful giver." In his second year he collected enough money to build a parsonage adjacent to the church.

About that time the town learned that Sylvia Akins, Peter's beautiful blond wife, was herself a cheerful giver and that not one but several members of the community had sown bountifully with her. She fled town, very pregnant but still beautiful, with the high school band director, the two of them one step ahead of being charged with unlawful fornication and the possession and use of marijuana. He didn't know what happened to her after that, only that she reportedly had gone to St. Louis. But he liked thinking there were women like her, and he admired her as much as he admired her husband. Peter Akins left town and left the ministry, his words seeming hollow now and tarnished as sounding brass to his disappointed congregation. He entered law school at the university, distinguished himself there, and turned his considerable talents from preaching about divine laws to interpreting man-made ones. He eventually went to Texas where he became a prosperous divorce attorney with offices in Dallas and Austin.

He still liked thinking about those days, and he guessed he owed Peter Akins a debt also. But now whenever anyone tried to talk to him about God, or Jesus—especially about Jesus—he had learned to run the other way. His life had been truer because of it. He saw no reason to change his mind about any of that now.

What more did he still want then? Nothing really. He had lived a good life and he could die without regret. Sometimes he wondered if it meant that he had merely lost all ambition. That wasn't it though. He still looked forward to each day, only now he accepted them as they came and for whatever each one brought. His expectations were more modest, his disappointments fewer and easier to bear. It was making sense of things that occupied his thoughts now. It was the stories that interested him most. The ones he had lived, and the ones he had made up in his head and thought about for so long that he couldn't remember any more whether he had lived them or only made them up. Or whether he had heard them from someone else, or read them somewhere. It didn't matter, they were his now, wherever they came from.

And they were all true, as true as he knew how to make them. For him they were the only truth that mattered. Not facts. That was someone else's truth. Beyond facts. He had gotten beyond facts long ago and there was no going back. The simple facts of our existence were merely the stage on which the real truth was acted out, the truth he found in the stories by which he was able to make sense of things. Facts were never the answer to any question. Real questions had no answer. That's what made them questions. Those who insisted on sticking to the facts never seemed to understand that it is all a story anyway, and it is all true. That was the only way to make sense out of it.

READERS GUIDE

1. What does the old dog represent to the man watching him out the window? What does he represent to the woman outside trying to run him off? Why does the man prepare to shoot the dog at the end? Why does the woman stop him?

2. What is happening to the man at the eighteenth hole? What kind of experience, mental and physical, is he having? When does he realize what is happening?

3. In what ways does the black house symbolize the lives of George and Karen? Is the new house any different? Does it change anything? Why does the narrator say that he is reassured and glad that George died in a rage?

4. Why do the voters find the campaign poster more significant and immediate than Sue Billings' accomplishments in office? What does the poster come to represent?

5. Why is Andy suddenly embarrassed and ashamed about what he has done? Has he been honest with himself about boxing a less capable opponent?

6. Why was his isolation from the crowd when he was on the court so important to Cody? Was it inevitable that the streak come to an end? What was Cody's problem with success and with the future?

7. What do the man and the woman have in common? How does each of them intensify and exaggerate the loneliness and frustrations of the other? Why does the man decline the woman's invitation to

accompany her to church, when he so obviously wants to accept?

8. Do you think Paul's understanding of his companion's needs and expectations was the same as her own, or has he only imagined what he wants to have happen?

9. Does Cynthia actually participate in any of the activities going on at the party, or does Paul merely imagine what he fears most? Can Paul ever be reassured of the truth?

10. Discuss some of the subtle ways that the mirrors on the walls produced the illusion of a distorted reality inside the house of mirrors. How does that illusion lead to greater candor and loss of inhibition?

11. What is the importance of the discovery that every age has its own distinctive aroma? Does it have any bearing on our understanding of history? What about such things as poverty, squalor and refugee camps, the smells of war and munitions?

12. Why are Ian Harris' perceptions of what goes on in the emergency room interesting and relevant? What are the parallels between William Sforza and William Kennedy?

13. What do each of the three men in the parables have in common? Why do you think the fourth man confides to his friends that he can find no fault with any of them? What do you suppose he means?

14. As the narrator reminisces about his life, why does storytelling become so important to him? What does he mean when he says "beyond facts?" Why do you suppose he says that real questions have no answers? What does that mean? In what way are the stories all true?

www.ingramcontent.com/pod-product-compliance
Lightning Source LLC
Chambersburg PA
CBHW011650010726
47496CB00012B/3021
* 9 7 8 1 6 3 2 9 3 3 1 0 2 *